The Stranger

There on the bluff she saw a man. A small figure, fifty yards off, standing dark against the flaming sky of the setting sun. Wild black grasses bent there in the wind, and the man's long coat rolled around his legs.

She knew who that man was.

And she was sure he was watching her.

The hair on her arms tingled, and she wanted to look away. But she held the dark man's gaze so that he would know she saw him. He wanted her to see him. She did. He wanted her to be afraid. He would not see her fear. She made up her mind to that.

But Colleen was afraid.

OTHER BOOKS YOU MAY ENJOY

Prairie
Whispers

FRANCES ARRINGTON

PUFFIN BOOKS

PUFFIN BOOKS
Published by the Penguin Group
Penguin Young Readers Group, 345 Hudson Street, New York, New York 10014, U.S.A.
Penguin Group (Canada), 10 Alcorn Avenue, Toronto,
Ontario, Canada M4V 3B2 (a division of Pearson Penguin Canada Inc.)
Penguin Books Ltd, 80 Strand, London WC2R 0RL, England
Penguin Ireland, 25 St Stephen's Green, Dublin 2, Ireland (a division of Penguin Books Ltd)
Penguin Group (Australia), 250 Camberwell Road, Camberwell, Victoria 3124,
Australia (a division of Pearson Australia Group Pty Ltd)
Penguin Books India Pvt Ltd, 11 Community Centre, Panchsheel Park, New Delhi - 110 017, India
Penguin Group (NZ), Cnr Airborne and Rosedale Roads, Albany, Auckland,
New Zealand (a division of Pearson New Zealand Ltd)
Penguin Books (South Africa) (Pty) Ltd, 24 Sturdee Avenue, Rosebank, Johannesburg 2196, South Africa

Registered Offices: Penguin Books Ltd, 80 Strand, London WC2R 0RL, England

First published by Philomel, a division of Penguin Putnam Books for Young Readers, 2003
Published by Puffin Books, a member of Penguin Young Readers Group, 2005

1 3 5 7 9 10 8 6 4 2

Patricia Lee Gauch, Editor
Text copyright © Frances Arrington, 2003
All rights reserved

THE LIBRARY OF CONGRESS HAS CATALOGED THE PHILOMEL EDITION AS FOLLOWS:
Arrington, Frances.
Prairie whispers / Frances Arrington.
cm.
Summary: Only twelve-year-old Colleen knows that her baby sister died just after she was born
and that Colleen put another baby in her place, until the baby's father shows up and
makes trouble for her and her family on the South Dakota prairie in the 1860s.
[1. Frontier and pioneer life—South Dakota—Fiction. 2. Family life—South Dakota—Fiction.
3. South Dakota—History—19th century—Fiction. 4. Babies—Fiction.] I. Title.
PZ7.A74337 Pr 2003
[Fic]—dc21
2002006698
ISBN 0-399-23975-8 (hardcover)

Puffin Books ISBN 0-14-240306-7

Printed in the United States of America

ACKNOWLEDGMENTS

I am grateful to the following people for sharing
their expertise and knowledge of the tall grass prairies
of South Dakota and of the people who settled there:
David Ode, South Dakota Game, Fish and Parks;
Herbert Hoover, University of South Dakota;
Carrie Lavarnway, Agricultural Heritage Museum, South Dakota;
Casey Kruse, Gavins Point Project, US Army Corps
of Engineers, South Dakota;
Dave Rambo, Blue Mound State Park, Minnesota;
Maxine Kinsley, South Dakota.

COLLEEN WAS HESITANT to approach the covered wagon. There could be sickness. She squinted, studying the wagon in the tall grasses over by the break. Wind rippled through the Indian grass, and bounced the seed heads against the wheels, but there was no sign of man nor beast.

She dawdled, watching the wagon, wondering who it was in that wagon over by the ravine. She edged slowly closer. Just watching.

Its canvas bulged, blown full by the heavy wind that now swirled Colleen's dark hair about her face. The wind escaped the hold of the canvas and rose in silence to the sky. And the canvas shuddered and flapped and put Colleen in mind of some small sailing ship blown across the land, white and pure and bright, to settle there in the tall grass less than a mile away from her own log house.

Colleen had spent the morning helping Ma, putting tomatoes in brine barrels, and then she had been set loose to walk two miles south to the river. The trip to the river was over now, more chores waited at home, and Colleen was in no hurry to get back.

She had not seen the wagon on her way to the river, having walked more than a mile down by the creek before climbing out of the ravine and following the foot trail alongside it on down to the river. Colleen's eyes traced the sweep of the prairie. There was an old cabin nearby. The one Ben Stockdale had lived in before he left for Lincoln County.

Colleen needed to go on home. Ma would scold if she took too long. She started walking, keeping to the edge of the ravine, and when she got closer, she saw the canvas on the wagon was not gleaming white. It was dirty, a dull warm nondescript color, not the bright clean thing the sun had made it from afar.

COLLEEN WALKED ON toward home, squinting now and then at the sun hovering far across the ravine. A topaz ball. It was later than she had figured.

She began to hurry. Soon she could see the cabin, the coppery light of the sun on the logs, her little brother's black dog darting from the corncrib to the cabin.

And she had promised Ma she'd grind corn. She started running. But Ma didn't like her charging in the cabin, so she stopped and walked. Like a civilized twelve-year-old.

Cinder bounded up and Colleen stooped down and scratched the dog's ears. "Where's Jeb?" she said, her eyes scanning the barnyard. The wind blew steady and there was no sign of Jeb.

Inside the cabin Colleen felt the collected heat of July filling the two rooms, and right then she felt something was wrong. Jeb met her at the door to the bedroom. "Ma's stomach hurts," he told her.

Colleen smiled at him. He sounded much too serious for someone only six years old.

Ma lay on the bed, on her side, her face shining, little beads of sweat on her forehead.

The baby? Colleen thought. The baby wasn't due for another month.

"Ma?" Colleen said.

Ma told Colleen she was all right. It would pass, just some cramps, they'd go away if she lay still . . .

Colleen didn't think so. Something wasn't right. Pa would be in Firesteel Creek till Wednesday. Maybe she should go get a neighbor.

Ma said no. She told Colleen to help by getting supper after her chores. "And remember the corn, Colleen," Ma said.

Colleen stood there for a moment.

"Go ahead," Ma said. "I'm fine."

So Colleen went to the little potbellied stove in the big room. She frowned and peeked back through the doorway at Ma. But she mustn't argue.

She got out the coffee grinder. She would grind the corn later.

Colleen took Jeb with her to feed the chickens and stable the horses. The wind had cooled and dark clouds were rolling about in the sky. Hurrying clouds, Colleen thought. Jeb ran ahead to the animals up a ways on the gentle north slope of prairie, but Colleen stood for a moment and watched the eastern sky. Thin, scraggly lightning streaked low to the ground, and far off Colleen heard the first faint rounds of heavy thunder.

BY MIDNIGHT COLLEEN would help her ma deliver the baby.

But it was not so simple as that.

The baby came too soon and lived less than an hour. Colleen knew as soon as she saw the baby; she was too small. Colleen put her in the cradle, kissed her on her forehead, and told her little brother the baby was asleep, to let her sleep.

"Ma already loved you," she whispered, smoothing the baby's dark hair. She stood there a minute, biting her bottom lip, and she dried her tears with the back of her hand.

Ma didn't know.

She was weak and drained, and would not answer the children. She did not even open her eyes. Colleen knitted her brows and studied her ma. She looked back at Jeb. "Maybe she lost too much blood . . . ," she said. She did not want to scare him. Maybe the blood was normal. She gave him a little smile. "You can help me," she told him. "You get some water." The children put wet rags on their ma's face and brought her to, but still Ma seemed to know little of what was going on.

"Ma's strong," Colleen told Jeb. "She'll get over this."

Colleen looked out the window, out the little glass panes into the black night.

The widow's farm was out there. Across the prairie going southeast. In the direction of the little river town. But closer. Only as far as the next break. And the widow was good birthing babies and helping after.

"Let's let her sleep," Colleen said. She pushed stray damp hairs off her ma's forehead. "I'm going to go get the Widow Jones."

Jeb crawled on the bed with Ma. "Don't faint again, Ma," Jeb said. He tried to give her water, but she lay pale and sleeping on the pillow. Jeb could hardly keep his own eyes open. Colleen looked quickly toward the cradle. Jeb would be asleep in a minute, and maybe it was best that way.

"Jeb," Colleen said. "The baby's asleep. Let her sleep. You stay by Ma." She grabbed Pa's old hat and a heavy drill jacket. "Stay by Ma, Jeb." Jeb's eyes were already closed.

Colleen ran from the cabin to the barn. She wished she had gone to the widow's earlier. But Ma had said no. A twelve-year-old girl did not belong out on a moonless night on the prairie, Ma had told her. Grown men could lose their way on such a night. It had happened to some man Pa knew. Some river valley man.

The rain was just beginning. Only a few drops yet, and the lightning was still miles off. Colleen saddled Shine.

She was afraid to ride the palomino too close to the ravine. In the rain he could slip. So she set out over the prairie heading toward the widow's, and Ma was right. She did not belong out here in this storm, out here in this blackness.

But Colleen was afraid for Ma, so she rode on and trusted the horse would go in the direction she had set him. Toward the river. Toward the Jones farm.

THE RAIN, SUDDENLY heavy, began driving in gusts, and Colleen and the horse were soaked before they were off the homestead. Colleen kept her eyes on the horizon, the silver-black prairie twitching, shivering with each pulse of lightning. And in that way she tried to judge her direction.

It was out of this wet world, out of this black rain that Colleen came upon the wagon again, the same wagon she had seen that afternoon, lit by the storm, straight in front of her. "Whoa! Whoa, Shine," she said. Shine stopped, and she patted his neck.

Maybe these strangers, surely these strangers, could help. Maybe they could go get the widow at least. And she could go back and wait at home with Ma.

The sky flashed. Colleen saw the abandoned Stockdale cabin over near the next ridge. She nudged the horse a few steps in that direction.

The lightning flickered, illuminating small outbuildings. A small barn. Were there people in there? Animals? She looked back to the wagon. Where were the people?

"Hello . . . ," she called. She waited for a minute and called out again. Her hair clung to her cheeks and rain dripped off the brim of Pa's old hat. She scraped the wet hair away from her face. Then she saw a slither of light from the back of the wagon.

The strangers were in the wagon. And they would help. She was certain. Colleen jumped down from the horse, ran to the rear of the wagon and beat on it, hit on it with her hands. She climbed up from the axle to the front seat. The rain slid off the wet canvas and splattered on her face.

"Hellooo?" Colleen called again. The canvas opened by itself, a gust of wind pushed it, and Colleen peered inside.

A lone candle on a trunk flickered. Colleen pushed the canvas all the way open and climbed inside, fighting with the heaviness of her sodden skirt. Inside she stopped. Even with the candle, it was dark inside. "Hello?" she said again softly.

The canvas behind her flapped, and Colleen pulled the drawstring trying to tie it shut and willed that single candle to keep burning. The canvas above her quivered, and somewhere inside the wagon rain was dripping. And Colleen heard something else. Someone whispered, and Colleen turned.

"Come, come here . . . ," came the whisper. Colleen

saw a woman, she thought, in a bed built into the corner of the wagon.

It was a young woman with shiny hair in the bed, and a dark-haired baby beside her.

Colleen was still for a moment. "I'm Colleen McCall," Colleen said, creeping forward. "I live just north of here. I came looking for help."

The young woman was smiling now. "And I was just praying for someone to come here," she said. "And help me."

E VEN IN THE CANDLELIGHT Colleen could see the skin around the woman's eyes was dark and her lips were the same chalky color as her face. Colleen bent over and looked down at her and the baby.

"How?" Colleen asked. "How can I help?"

"Just listen to me," the woman whispered. And Colleen nodded.

The wagon woman's name was Mary Kathleen O'Brien. She and her husband were on their way further west. Into the hinterlands. The Fort Pierre area. But she was pregnant and she had told her husband she needed time to stop and rest for a day or so. Her husband had left for Chouteau Creek late that afternoon. He was a gambler. He could be gone for days.

"Oh!" Colleen put her hand to her mouth. Colleen knew about Chouteau Creek. A good ways on down the river over near the Yankton Sioux reservation, like the little river town where her family went for mail. But different. Pa said it was no place for women or children.

"No," Mary Kathleen said. She had told him it wasn't

time for the baby to come, to go on then, before the time for the baby. The woman closed her eyes.

Colleen looked helplessly about the wagon, wondered what to do. The wagon woman grabbed Colleen's wrist then. The coldness of the woman's hand surprised Colleen, and she looked back at her.

The young woman had had her baby earlier, by herself, after her husband left, and she had been glad. She had wanted him to be gone when she had the baby.

Outside the rain fell on the dark grass, seeped into the warm earth. Inside the wagon too, the rain seeped, and Colleen turned her head and stared momentarily into a dark corner at the sound of the storm dripping there.

And so at first Colleen did not understand what the wagon woman was asking her to do.

The wagon woman was begging Colleen to take her baby girl, should she die. Colleen opened her mouth but closed it again.

She was *dying*? This woman? Colleen stared at Mary Kathleen O'Brien. She *couldn't* be dying. Colleen had to get help for *Ma*. What about Ma?!

The wagon woman did not know about Colleen's ma. She kept on . . . She had married her husband with little thought . . . a mistake. And then there was the trip west she wasn't ready to undertake. . . . From time to time her husband would say things that chilled her heart . . . then things had happened. He would change. In a heartbeat. Like a wounded animal, the woman said. She had become afraid of him. And now, she was afraid for her baby.

"He'd hurt the child for certain. I swear on my own mother's grave, he would," the woman insisted. Colleen must never let the man have this baby. "Never. If I die, you'll take the baby," the young woman begged.

Colleen shook her head. "You won't die. You're not dying," Colleen whispered.

"Promise . . . ," the woman said. And all Colleen thought was that she needed to get help for Ma. Now!

"Promise!" the woman demanded. And Colleen promised.

Iwill. I'll take her," Colleen said, glancing over at the tiny baby wrapped in a blanket beside its mother. "And I won't tell your husband. No matter what," Colleen added. She could do that. Ma'd want her to help. It seemed not a bad promise to make. And the woman let go of her wrist.

Colleen was afraid. This woman could hardly breathe. Colleen didn't know what to do to help her, to help her to breathe better. *She didn't know.* And Colleen had to leave, *she had to go get help for Ma.*

Colleen bit her lips, and tried to think.

"I know," Colleen began eagerly. The candlelight flickered across the canvas walls. "Don't you worry. . . . I can get someone to come help you. My ma, she's sick too. But I can get help for you too." Widow Jones would want to help. It was a good plan.

But the wagon woman did not seem to hear.

She was talking again, between breaths, and Colleen tried to listen to her words, tried to make sense of them, tried to remember them. *The war back east. Her husband in the war. A box.* They were important words, Colleen knew that, but Colleen did not listen well; she could not stop thinking about her ma.

Colleen hadn't thought Mary Kathleen O'Brien would really die. It was all over before she had a chance to think. First the wagon woman was looking at Colleen, her green eyes sparkling in the candlelight, and then she closed them and she just stopped breathing. The black wind cried outside the wagon. And the wagon creaked and moaned. Yet it seemed so still there inside. So still.

Colleen stared at her. She looked so thin, so young. This wagon woman, she had prayed for someone to come. And Colleen had been that someone. Mary Kathleen O'Brien had hung on and waited. And now just as Colleen gave her word, the wagon woman had closed her eyes and was gone.

"Mary Kathleen? . . . Are you all right?" Colleen asked, but she knew better. She felt her wrist for a pulse. But it was no use.

A bolt of lightning. And thunder. Colleen's face swung upwards staring into the dark, wondering if the canvas above her would tear open, and the wind shook the wagon so that Colleen truly thought the wagon might blow over. And maybe then they would all fall into the ravine.

Colleen tried to remember what she had been told.

There was a strongbox, a heavy metal thing, on the trunk. She was supposed to take that. It had money in it for the baby. Colleen threw the box out the back of the wagon, and scrambled out to tie it to Shine's saddle.

Climbing back in the wagon, Colleen picked up the candle in one hand and went to the baby. She loosened its blanket so she could wrap it tightly for the trip. The baby opened her eyes and kicked her little round legs. Colleen smiled for a moment and leaned closer.

But how could she carry this baby? She looked around the dark wagon. She couldn't get on the horse *holding* the baby. Tie a basket on the saddle horn? The horse could spook.

A loud clap of thunder rattled her thoughts. Colleen frowned. She would have to carry the baby. She would have to walk back home and carry the baby. So in the flickering candlelight, Colleen hurried and readied the baby for the trip. Her eyes darted about. The woman had said to take a gold watch for the baby . . . where? On the bed. She snatched up the watch. Was there anything else? No. That was all, she thought.

She looked back quickly. "Bye," she whispered. "Bye, Mary Kathleen O'Brien. I will keep your baby safe . . . I will." Colleen bit her lips and blew out the candle and turned and then clambered out the back and reached up for the baby.

And all the time Colleen remembered these words the woman said. *It was providence.* It was providence that had brought her here in this wet, deep darkness to save this baby.

COLLEEN PULLED PA'S old hat further down on her head and with the baby in one arm, she took Shine's reins.

The rain was easing, distant lightning quivered behind breaks in the clouds. Low to the horizons. And the pitch grasslands swept under them away to the edge of the world.

She had better go home, go back and wait the storm out. She doubted now she could find her way to the widow's. Home was north beside the same ravine. Home was a mile away if she could get there.

But Colleen's fear of the ravine, of Shine slipping on the wet, slick grass and falling into the ravine, gave her pause. The horse was skittish as it was. So she moved Shine away from the ravine, out into the midst of the prairie.

Once, while faint pulses of lightning trembled in the distance, Colleen saw what looked to be a giant crouching cat. It took her by surprise, and she stared at it, took it to be clouds at the edge of the horizon.

Still she stared at it. The lightning hit closer again. Split seconds of flat, unearthly light. Then black again. And thunder. Thunder in the willows, in the grass, in the sky.

And then a bolt of lightning split the air so close, it left behind the smell of sulphur.

"Easy, Shine," Colleen said. "Just lightning . . ."

But Shine bolted. Colleen watched the horse run off, quickly disappearing into the night. She clutched the baby and ran a little ways after him, hoping he would stop soon, but something tripped her and she almost fell.

"Whoa . . . whoa, Shine," she called. But he was gone, and Colleen was left standing holding the baby on the dark land, hardly knowing what direction she faced. She started walking and walked for a half hour blindly with only the lightning and the dark.

She looked around. Now she had no idea where they might be.

It seemed quieter somehow now. Still. The faint smell of sulphur lingered in the air. Light rain started again. Colleen took the hat off and held it over the baby as she walked through the wet grasses. And for a long time Colleen struggled to believe she was almost there, almost home.

Finally she stopped.

The baby whimpered, made tiny cries. "It's all right,

little baby." Colleen adjusted the baby into her other arm and searched the night for a light from some homestead. She did not move. She waited there in the stillness, looking, listening.

The storm was moving on. Large, scattered drops from the black sky now. She heard them hitting the grasses around her, and the wind was gentle, all but stopped. Still Colleen waited. She watched for the shimmers of lightning to show her the land, and then she turned and began to walk.

T HE CABIN WAS DARK. A candle stub, waiting to die out, cast a small glow on the unhewn walls. Colleen found her ma and little Jeb there, found them still sleeping, just as she had left them.

Jeb was sound asleep, the blanket pulled up under his nose, his nut-brown hair tousled on the pillow. But Ma was still very weak. Colleen went to her bed holding tight to Mary Kathleen's baby. Ma was still drifting in and out of a deep sleep-like state, and Ma did not even seem to understand that Colleen had left. That Colleen wanted to go get help.

The baby, Mary Kathleen's baby, squirmed in the wrappings. Colleen took the wet blanket away and looked at the baby. Her little arms reached wildly in the air. She made an excited sound like she was going to cry but she stopped. Colleen smiled and dried her off and wrapped her in a clean blanket and lay her between Jeb and Ma on the bed.

"Now, how's that?" she asked. "Better?"

The clock ticked slowly on in the quiet.

It was Ma's baby now.

Suddenly Colleen looked to the cradle. Her eyes fixed there for a moment. Her throat became tight. She walked over, picked up the tiny, bluish baby sister, and while she held her she looked back to Mary Kathleen O'Brien's baby.

Take this little one back to Mary Kathleen O'Brien. Bury her with Mary Kathleen. In her arms.

The thought surprised Colleen. Where had such a thought come from? Surely she hadn't thought such a thing.

And yet she looked down at the little thing in her arms, and there was some comfort in that thought. She put the tiny baby down and went and sat beside Ma.

And Colleen asked her ma was that the thing to do, to switch the babies, to bury this little one with Mary Kathleen? "Then it wouldn't be buried alone, Ma," Colleen said. "And we can keep Mary Kathleen's baby like she wanted . . . Is that the thing to do?

"Is it . . . Ma?"

Ma said something Colleen could not make out. Ma did not seem to hear Colleen. She could not answer her.

Colleen decided on her own.

She decided to bury the tiny blue baby with Mary Kathleen O'Brien. She wrapped the baby tightly in a small blanket and placed it in a basket. She left the cabin again. In the early morning, before any blue of day. She left carrying the tiny blue baby.

There would be no telling. There would be no turning back.

Out over the land, out far over the horizon, tiny bright stars began to light the sky, and all that was left now from the storm was wet drops falling from the roof.

Shine was back. He stood with his head down near the barn.

Colleen carried the tiny baby, and led Shine to the barn to dry and bed him down. She hung the lantern beside the stalls and got the horse's blanket. Shine was tired and cold. She would switch to Bayboy for the trip.

After taking the saddle off Shine, when Colleen was rubbing him down, she realized the strongbox was gone. The box Mary Kathleen had told her to take. She looked at the saddle for a moment and glanced around the barn. She did not see it.

The tall grasses of the untamed prairie flickered in her mind's eye. The far horizons. The box was out there. Somewhere. It must have fallen off when Shine ran. Maybe she could find it though, she told herself, and she put it out of her mind. It didn't seem important.

She still had the gold watch. She grabbed it out of her pocket and ran to stuff it in her trunk in the corner of the barn.

Colleen walked leading the horse and carrying her baby sister to Mary Kathleen's wagon, crawled into it and left her there beside Mary Kathleen O'Brien. She stood there looking at the two of them, her fingers to her mouth, her eyes beginning to burn. "You go to Heaven together," she whispered. "The two of you." And it made her glad that at least her baby sister had someone to be her ma.

Colleen rode Bayboy on across the prairie through the tall, wet grasses to the Jones farm.

The light in the east was just breaking. One of the widow's grown sons said he and his brother would see to the woman in the wagon and her baby, would take care of the burying at the cemetery down near the Missouri.

Colleen said she wanted to go, and asked them to tell her when it would be. She did not say it would be her baby sister's burying . . .

The widow, a tall woman, white hair, dark eyes and brows, walked straight to the wagon. She stopped to look closely at one wheel. The older son stooped down and looked too, and Colleen heard only quiet words between them.

Colleen tied Bayboy to the widow's buckboard and rode back home with the Widow Jones and on the way the widow asked Colleen about the woman in the wagon and about her baby.

Colleen stared ahead at the ridge of tall grass and tried to choose the right words. "The woman was real sick. She had the baby yesterday—no, today . . . I can't remember . . ."

"Imagine! Poor woman. Who was she? Did she tell you where she came from?"

"No . . . I mean, she didn't say much of anything. She was too sick . . . except she told me her name. Mary Kathleen O'Brien."

"What about the baby? Was it already dead when you got there?"

Colleen shook her head. "No . . . but . . . then it died . . . and the woman, she said she wanted to be buried with it, with her baby."

"We'll have to locate her family . . . her husband. He must've come out here with her. What did she say about him?"

The husband? She was supposed to hide the baby from the husband. Should she talk about the husband?

"Nothing . . . She didn't talk about him. Maybe she said he was gone somewhere . . . and . . . I don't think she said. She didn't say . . ."

They were to be only the first of Colleen's lies. And Colleen felt funny about them, afraid of the lies, afraid she could not remember what she had said. Because it was not the truth.

And afraid of the bigness of the lies.

She could not tell Widow Jones that she had the wagon woman's baby at her own cabin, that the baby with Mary Kathleen O'Brien now was her own baby sister born too soon. She could not say that.

That little baby, Colleen thought. It had grasped her finger. She had to protect that baby. She had promised.

The buckboard rolled on, groaning its way across the prairie, and she watched the wind tracing its fingers over the grass.

MA'S ALL BETTER," Jeb said. Ma's bell-chimes jangled outside in the wind, and Colleen opened her eyes. Dried squash hung from the rafters above her. And Jeb and Cinder were staring in her face.

"You slept till noon," the widow said. "Come have something to eat."

"Oh, thank you!" Colleen said, and she scrambled out of her small bed in the corner of the big room. She raced Jeb barefooted across the split log floor to Ma's room.

Ma and the baby were both asleep. Colleen grinned at Jeb, her finger up over her lips, and they crept closer. Ma did look better. And the beautiful baby. She smiled at the baby. *Providence* had sent them that baby.

Colleen heard voices out the window. The widow and her grown son. Colleen could see them from the small window.

They didn't know.

Colleen bit her fingernail and looked around the room. At Ma and the baby. At the little braided rag rug by the bed . . . and something else . . . something under the bed. A paper.

Colleen stooped down and picked it up. Did it fall from the baby's blanket last night?

DEAR KIND STRANGER, it began.

Mary Kathleen wrote this.

Colleen glanced out the window. They were still there.

PLEASE TAKE MY BABY AND LOVE HER. HER FATHER FRIGHTENS ME, AND I FEAR FOR MY DEAR BABY'S SAFETY. PLEASE KEEP MY BABY FROM HIM.

It was signed MARY KATHLEEN O'BRIEN.

Colleen stared at the paper in her hand.

She wrote this for me . . . before I came.

Colleen ran to the big room. Her little bed sat high above a storage chest in the far corner. She ran there and pushed the letter through a loose seam in her straw tick, pushed it deep into the hay.

It was quiet and she heard her own breathing, and she almost heard her heart.

Just before the widow's son left, Colleen put a cool, wet rag on Ma's forehead. The widow had said Ma did not have a fever. But it's what Ma did when she and Jeb were sick. The rag would make Ma feel better.

Colleen watched the widow as she came in. She had heard the widow and her son talking about the old Stockdale place, about the woman and the baby there, and they said the burying would be late that afternoon.

"I'd like to go," Colleen whispered, turning her face from Ma to the Widow Jones, "to the buryin' . . . I'd like to go." The widow looked long at Colleen, and Colleen felt uneasy.

"With your ma having been through this difficult birth, Colleen?" the widow asked.

"I . . . I thought she was all right . . . all right now," Colleen said. Her eyes darted to Ma. Ma was going to be well now, wasn't she? Colleen looked back at Widow Jones.

"You'll do best to stay right here," Widow Jones said.

No, Colleen thought. Not if Ma really is all right. She stood up by the bed, her dark eyes moving back and forth from the widow to Ma.

She tried to look calm.

The widow didn't know providence had sent her, Colleen McCall, to that woman's wagon. The widow had no notion that it was Colleen's own baby sister being buried. The widow didn't know it, but she, Colleen McCall, *was too* going to the buryin'. It was only fitting.

Ma stirred in the bed, and Colleen took Ma's hand in both of hers. Ma looked over at Widow Jones.

"I'm fine, Hannah, just tired," Ma said, opening her eyes and turning over on her side toward the baby. She smiled. "It'll do Colleen good to go. She gets these notions in her head sometimes, feeling for unfortunate folks."

Colleen sat down on the bed beside Ma, beaming, and Ma reached for the baby.

"Look at this girl, would you?" Ma said, pushing the blanket further open beside the baby's face. The baby's tiny hands were balled into little fists. Her eyes were a dark, beautiful blue. Colleen reached out a finger and touched the baby's soft little arm, and Colleen smiled at her ma and at the warm little baby.

And though Colleen needed to tell Ma what all had happened . . . and she would tell her, it was only right . . . with the widow woman there, Colleen felt she couldn't. It all had to be a secret, didn't it? From the widow. From everyone. So that the wagon man, Mary Kathleen's husband, would not know. And so for now, Ma thought this baby was her own baby.

All of it was left unsettled, and Colleen's heart beat hard and fast thinking about that and about what she had to say when the widow left.

THE WIDOW JONES stayed with Ma until around four. Colleen and Jeb and Cinder stood near the doorway watching her. She hung a dried cooking pot on its peg on the wall with other utensils near Colleen's little bed.

"Let your ma get some rest," the widow warned Colleen and Jeb both before she left. Jeb watched her, his brown eyes big, and nodded his head seriously, and Colleen said yes, they would. "Lots of rest," Colleen repeated.

Colleen left for the burying soon after. Ma was asleep. Colleen didn't think she ought to wake her.

The burying was on a bluff down near the river not far from the small river settlement where Colleen went for mail.

There was only a scattering of folks there. No one had known the woman in the wagon, and few people had even returned to the county since the Indian trouble the year before. The preacher was not due thereabouts till sometime in August, so the widow's second son, Mark, who had a calling, said the words at the grave.

"Accept our sister and this little one into your kingdom, Lord . . ."

It was over almost as soon as it began, and Colleen found Shine grazing out past the cemetery. The sun would be setting soon. It cast its red glow over the river and beyond, and Colleen looked out over the wide flat Missouri, far across to the hills on the Nebraska side. A small steamboat stirred there near the edge of the river. Maybe stopped for wood.

Colleen strained her eyes watching. Probably the last she'd see of the boats for a long while. The river would be too low in August. Colleen wished it weren't so. She liked to see the little steamboats passing on the great river.

"You let me know if your pa isn't back tomorrow," the widow said suddenly, startling Colleen, and she looked over her shoulder at the Widow Jones walking her way. The widow straightened the cuffs on her sleeves and studied Colleen. "I'll be back before long either way, and check on your ma." The widow glanced toward the windswept bluffs upriver, and Colleen waited.

Widow Jones continued, "Your ma said your pa was hauling freight to some militia group? Up the James?"

Colleen shook her head. "Up to Firesteel Creek . . . to that fort that's up there."

"Your ma's baby was right early."

"Some . . . Some early. We didn't expect it for . . . for a while yet," Colleen answered. And Colleen's heart changed its beat.

She thinks the baby should be smaller.

Colleen stood there quiet, cautious. She didn't want to answer the widow's questions, but she had to say something.

"You let me know about your pa now," the widow said to Colleen. Colleen nodded and the widow woman walked off toward her wagon where the elder son and his wife stood.

Colleen watched her go. *Don't come back. Ma is all right now.* She wished she could say it. She always used to enjoy the widow's visits. Minding other people's business made for some interesting conversations. But not now. Now she did not want the widow around.

Colleen straightened her old straw hat on her head and ran toward Shine. From the top of the bluff, she looked over to the settlement further down river.

Hardly a town at all. A hotel, a blacksmith, and a couple of other establishments. In the distance she noticed a rider heading that way, and she wondered when Mary Kathleen O'Brien's husband would return. For she knew he would, and the thought made her nervous.

She took a last look at the river, wide and braided, before turning Shine to go.

Well, Colleen told herself, when the O'Brien man does come, no need to fear. He does not know.

The beautiful baby at home belonged to her family now.

COLLEEN CROSSED TWO miles of rolling prairie. There she joined up with the small foot trail near the edge of the break. It wound through shrubs and tall grasses and other growth and would lead to home. Maybe she could find some ripe currants in the break, take them home to Ma and Jeb.

She'd best not stop though till she was closer to home and then see how the light was. So Colleen rode on and soon she came to Mary Kathleen's wagon.

She pulled back on Shine's reins. He reared a bit. "Whoa, Shine," Colleen said softly. She circled Shine and pulled him to a stop.

It was quiet. Just the rustle of grasses bowing in their endless dance with the wind. There was no sign of the husband having returned.

Colleen knew she needed to get on home. At home pans of milk waited for her to skim the cream off the top. And at home, Ma waited. Not knowing.

She would have to tell Ma.

Colleen did not want to do that. And the man was not here. He could come back anytime though. Maybe she should stop here, look for that box. This might be her last chance to search here for that box.

An ax. There against the wagon. She didn't remember an ax before. Her gaze flicked toward the old cabin. No one.

So Colleen got off the horse and looked around, combing the ground, the grasses, looking for the strongbox that she had lost in the storm.

It would be dark soon. Colleen heard Shine neighing, and a meadowlark's call reminding her she had to get home. She could not find the box now. It probably wasn't around there anyway. "He'll leave soon," Colleen told Shine. "He'll go away."

She decided she would come back though just to make sure.

Ma would let her. Ma sent her often for mail. News of the war. News from Pennsylvania. From their people back east.

Colleen would go down to the settlement for mail. And on her way she would make sure the wagon man was gone.

At home Jeb came running out to meet Colleen. "Ma's up!" he yelled. "And Cinder likes the baby!"

Colleen laughed. A tiny flame glimmered at the window, and Colleen heard Ma inside singing. She grinned at Jeb and ran to the door.

"Ma!" she said, stopping there in the doorway.

"That's the song you used to sing to make Jeb go to sleep." Colleen ran over to Ma and the baby.

"Look at her, Colleen." Ma arranged the blanket softly around the baby's face. "Isn't she a wonder?" The little baby moved her arms about and put her hand in her mouth.

Colleen beamed at Ma and nodded.

The widow had left supper for them. And after Colleen ran back out to stable Shine, she started to warm the cornbread. She went to the wood box behind the stove. And then she looked back suddenly at Ma.

And she knew it was time.

It was time. *Right now,* Colleen told herself. Time to tell her.

"Ma . . . ," she began, still standing where she had stopped near the wood box.

Ma had just told Jeb to bring the candle from the window over to the cupboard, and she looked at Colleen and smiled. Jeb jumped up off the floor.

Colleen waited till Jeb got the candle settled on the cupboard. And she waited while Jeb hung over the side of the chair and looked at the baby's little hand wildly moving up and down. "She's going to grab my hair and pull it!" Jeb grinned.

"I hardly think so," Ma laughed. "At least not yet."

She looked over at Colleen, who stood clutching her right hand in the left. "Colleen?" Ma said.

Colleen shook her head and smiled weakly at her ma. *Ma's so pale* . . . she began to tell herself. But it was no good. Colleen knew Ma was going to be well now. There was no reason to wait.

"Won't your pa be surprised to see this new child waiting when he gets home," Ma said, and Jeb nodded and laughed.

Colleen stood over by the wall. She heard the soft bell tones of a bird, a killdeer she thought, outside somewhere. The candlelight flickered around on their faces and Colleen felt a sinking feeling in her chest.

But she mustn't feel that way. Ma and Pa would understand what she did. Ma and Pa would still love this baby. They would be glad to help Mary Kathleen O'Brien keep this baby safe too. Just like her.

It's time, she told herself again. And she really tried to find the words.

It's not . . . your . . . baby.

No. She couldn't say that.

Our baby died. Was that what she was supposed to say? It was, wasn't it? But Colleen didn't want to say that.

Even when she thought those words, her heart raced. She went over to the little potbellied stove and traced her finger along its edge. She needed to help Ma by doing the cream. She needed to warm supper, and she started but soon her hands fell beside her, and she turned her head and looked at Ma and Jeb.

Jeb was bent over, his face sideways on level with the baby's. He was grinning and eyeing the baby . . . Ma could not take her eyes from the little face either. She thinks it's hers, Colleen thought. She turned back to the stove.

Not now, she thought. *Surely now is not the right time.*

It was not true. Colleen knew that. The truth was she did not have the heart to tell Ma right then. I'll tell her in the morning, Colleen told herself.

But morning came and Colleen did not tell.

COLLEEN SPENT THE NEXT morning in the garden. Her work, a pile of weeds, lay scattered about her bare feet in the dirt beside the hoe. She stood, both hands over her eyes, watching. Just south of Paul Russert's cabin, past the draw there, she saw a tiny speck against the far far sky. A couple more homesteads dotted the landscape that way. She watched the direction of this wagon. She figured it was her pa.

"Ma!" Colleen called. "Jeb!" Colleen ran to the door of the cabin. "He's coming! . . . Pa's home!" and Colleen ran back outside. Her hair, pulled smoothly back that morning, now tousled, coming loose in the hot wind. Tiny strands of it caught in her eyes. She brushed them away, and she kept watching.

She would tell Pa what had happened. Right off. And he would tell Ma. Pa, being grown, would know the right way, the right words, to tell Ma.

Jeb dashed out the door, and Ma followed with the baby in her arms.

No, Ma . . . don't bring out the baby . . . not till I tell him.

Jeb ran off into the swirling tall grass toward the wagon, shouting the news. Laughing and shouting the news. "The baby, Pa! Ma had the baby!" he cried.

It seemed odd to watch Jeb running ahead, Colleen thought. Ordinarily she would have been far ahead of Jeb running to tell news such as this.

But now.

Colleen glanced back toward the cabin and Ma. Colleen would have to wait now. She'd have to wait for the time when she could tell Pa. She stood there in the garden, feeling strangely separate.

She felt the same when Ma, smiling under the churning, white-clouded sky, told Pa what had happened. Colleen led the horses away to the barn, and she looked back at her tall, lanky pa, there with Ma and the beautiful new baby, there with Jeb and Cinder jumping around them.

Words drifted in the sun. Her ma's words. Her pa's. ". . . don't know what I would have done without her . . . can count on our Colleen . . ."

And Colleen knew some of what Ma said was not true. But Colleen kept on walking with the horses toward the barn. She did not want to hear more.

Inside Colleen sat on the bench at the table with Jeb. Pa was not much of a talker, a quiet man, but Ma and Jeb had plenty to say. Pa's eyes sparkled when Ma gave him the baby to hold. "Well. We're outnumbered, boy," Pa told Jeb.

Pa looked at Colleen, his eyes smiling, and Jeb grinned at his pa and the baby.

They named the baby Bonnie. And Colleen had to jump up then and run around the table and look at Bonnie and laugh at the wonderful little ways she moved.

Cinder barked and Bonnie looked startled, an innocent, wide-eyed look. "That's Cinder, Bonnie," Pa said.

Pa thinks this is his baby girl, Colleen thought.

Colleen dragged a chair to the table and sat next to Pa listening to the talk. Pa had the freighting money. Pa and Ma talked about maybe getting a couple more cattle, for the foundation herd. Someday the farm would become a ranch. The two of them talked on and on.

There's no time, Colleen thought. No time to tell Pa. But of course, she knew there was time. If she made it.

Stop . . . I need to tell you all something about the baby.

She could say it right then, right then.

She should.

If she did, though, it felt like she would choke, like she would smother.

After supper, she told herself. After supper she would tell Pa.

She sat there in the cabin listening to her family. She sat there with her secret. Separate again.

FTER THE NOON MEAL, Colleen worked again in the garden, her heart pounding a heavy beat that seemed a part of her now. A strong wind came in from the west. Colleen stood up straight and looked across the grasslands to the far and endless sky. The afternoon went on.

Pa went to check the stock, Jeb following along, and Colleen watched them till they were most a quarter of a mile out on the east ridge and then she ran after them, out into the open grasses past the fields of Indian corn. And into the tall native grasses.

She would tell Pa now.

I have something to say, she would tell him. Something important. And if Jeb wanted to stay and listen, that was all right. It wasn't Jeb she was afraid to tell.

"Pa!" she called. She began running toward them. Pa and Jeb turned and she kept on running, and the tall grass heads danced all about them in the sun. She did not want to do this. But she had to.

Colleen stopped just a hundred feet short of Pa and Jeb. They were waiting for her, watching her.

And she stopped running and stood there and wondered. Would Pa and Ma think they could keep the baby? With never a word to the man who was her real father? Pa and Ma? God-fearing people. Good people, but strict. Law-abiding. Pa and Ma went by the law. Would they go by the law now?

She took a sudden deep breath, and she wondered if maybe, if maybe she should say nothing?

Pa and Jeb waited on the ridge. "Colleen?" Pa said. Colleen ran to catch up, and they walked out on the ridge where they could see the cattle grazing beyond.

And Colleen decided right then she had better hide the watch, hide it till later. Until she knew what she was going to do. She looked back toward the barn. The watch was in the burlap bag, deep in her trunk in the barn where she had put it that night. It was not safe there. Anyone could find it.

And she better get rid of that letter, too. The one that she had hidden in her bed.

Pa said he was going down to town to the blacksmith's. Jeb wanted to go and Pa said he could.

"You come too, Colleen," Jeb said. Colleen looked at Jeb squinting up at her.

Even little Jeb could find the watch. Even he knew that was where she had always kept things.

"I better stay here. Ma might need me to help with Bonnie," she told him.

Back at the barn, Colleen strayed about the barnyard watching till Pa and Jeb disappeared heading southeast for town across the prairie, and then she ran to the barn to get the gold watch.

COLLEEN STOOD A MOMENT in the warmth of the barn staring at the old chest. She had always kept her treasures there, even back in Pennsylvania, before they had come here two years ago, to settle in this land of wind and sky.

But she could not keep this watch here.

She left for the ravine with a cracked crock pot from the root cellar and the watch.

She stopped at the rim. Her eyes wandered, picking their way down. Buffalo berries, wild plums. The creek at the bottom. She looked back at the cabin before starting down. She found a spot near the bottom. Sandbar willow and false indigo had taken root there. If she buried the watch there, it wouldn't wash away.

Colleen pulled the gold watch out of her pocket. It lay in her hand shining, sparkling in the sun. Heavy and cool. She pushed at a gold nub on the side. The watch popped open, and Colleen looked curiously at it. Beautiful Roman numerals and watch hands lay under smooth clean glass.

She dug her hole with a broken piece of crockery she'd brought to cut into the earth and buried the watch in the crock pot.

Surely this was what she was supposed to do . . .

Right now she had to make sure nothing bad happened to the baby, and right now she didn't care what else she was supposed to do. She'd promised Mary Kathleen O'Brien she'd keep the baby safe, and Mary Kathleen O'Brien had died believing that was what she would do. There was surely no promise more important than one made to somebody dying. And keeping that promise is what she, Colleen McCall, was going to do.

And then Colleen scooted on down to the bottom of the ravine where she folded her arms and paced about in the cool shallow creek.

She just might never tell anybody.

Cottonwoods and willows edged the bank of the creek. Their leaves gleamed and rippled, alive in the prairie wind. Colleen glanced up to the top of the ravine to a hawk in the blue of the summer sky, and that was when she saw something. Something out of the corner of her eye, at the top of the ravine on the other side. A dark figure, a rider on a horse? But when she looked again, there was nothing there and Colleen wondered if she had really seen it. If anything had really been there at all.

IN THE MORNING, Colleen went with her pa riding, looking for a stray. Ever so often, Pa would let her go with him looking for lost steers, and more times than not, Colleen would spot the wayward animal tucked away in a thicket, or lazing in stands of cordgrass that grew here and there near the ravines, trying to escape the blaze of the sun.

The day was clear and bright. The colors of the prairie were deep. Creeks that fed into the river ambled their way south in crooked trails across the prairie. Down in the break, thousands of sparkling leaves on the cottonwoods quivered in the wind.

Pa and Colleen stopped the horses near the top of the ravine. The creek twisted and ran for a short length eastward.

"There!" Colleen said, pointing. The steer stood almost hidden behind bushes on the slope of the ravine.

Pa squinted down across the creek. "I believe you're right," he said. Pa smiled at her, and called her his eagle-eyed girl. Like he always did.

• • •

Later, after the stray was home, Colleen carried water to the cabin for Ma and water to the hens and ran down to the creek to get a bucket Jeb had left down there. But when she was following the little path through the wild grass back to the cabin, she stopped.

A stranger was there, at their cabin, a man on a horse.

Cavalry? A scout? Maybe just someone patrolling, she hoped. But when she walked closer, she knew it was not cavalry. By the time she got to the cabin she knew that. It was the wagon man.

Colleen stood there with Jeb listening to Pa and the man talking, and she saw Ma back by the cabin near where her big washbasin hung outside the door.

". . . There's some Sioux milling around . . . most're peaceful . . . ," Pa was saying. "We see them sometimes. They pass through here . . . over to the Yankton reservation . . . over past Chouteau Creek Station." Colleen didn't hear everything he said. She couldn't think.

She squinted at the wagon man, a soft beard, neatly trimmed, wide-set eyes, a nice face, Colleen thought. That is why Mary Kathleen O'Brien was fooled.

Please leave. Just leave . . . Colleen thought.

But the man did not leave.

Bonnie began to cry. Little wails drifted out from the cabin, and when they did not stop, Ma went inside.

The man got down off his horse. "That's some fine beef you got over there."

Colleen scratched an insect bite on her wrist.

". . . Government's buying livestock for the tribes," Pa said. ". . . It's a sure market, hard cash."

The man smiled and looked out to the cattle on the ridge. Colleen sidled toward the cabin door and slipped inside.

But Ma did not need her inside. "You go on back out, Colleen. That's the man whose wife and child died. The woman you talked to the night of the storm. You know that man must want to know about his wife. His child. He must have questions."

Colleen did not budge. She stared at Ma.

"Go on," Ma said. "I've got Bonnie."

"Ma . . . I don't know what to say to that man. His wife *died*."

"It's all right, Colleen. Just tell him the truth."

So Colleen went back outside and crossed her arms and stood backed up to the log wall next to the door, watching.

". . . Was told down at the hotel that a young girl and a woman buried my wife," the man was saying.

"The woman would be the Widow Jones. The widow and her boys saw to the buryin'," Pa said. "The girl, that was Colleen. Colleen found your wife."

And Pa turned and motioned for her to come. "This is Colleen."

T HE MAN HAD BEEN to the grave. Now he wanted
to know things. And Colleen tried to answer. Some
things were missing from the wagon, and he wanted to
know what Colleen knew.

It made Colleen uneasy, the man asking her questions. She heard only pieces of what he said. A strongbox. Hundred. A hundred what? Dollars?

Colleen told about the storm and how his wife had
had the baby before Colleen got there, and Colleen lied
and said she took nothing from the wagon. And that lie
was not easy. But the lie about the baby was worse. He
asked about the baby. How was the baby when she got
there? How was his wife? Colleen stared at him.

And she did not know.

Because, because his baby, Bonnie, was alive and
well. But the story was, the story was that this man's
baby was the one that died. Colleen tried to think. She
couldn't.

"The baby?" she heard herself saying. Colleen flicked
her glance to the cabin, to the clapboards above the logs,
to Ma's bell chimes up under the eaves.

What had she told the widow? What had she told the widow early that morning? She could not remember. Maybe it hadn't come up. Maybe she hadn't said anything about that.

"Colleen, tell Mr. O'Brien how they were, how his wife and baby were when you got there," Pa said. Colleen saw Ma just outside the door now, her hand shading her eyes. Colleen looked back at the man, her little finger up at her lips.

"She was alive," Colleen stammered. "Your wife, but . . . she was real weak, real sick. . . . She knew she was dying . . ." But what about the baby? What about the baby? Was there a right answer? Was she supposed to say it was alive then or that it had already died before she got there? What had she told the widow?

Colleen looked up at Pa and back at Mr. O'Brien.

"The baby was already dead," she said. Already dead, she repeated in her mind. *Already dead*. She kept looking right at Mr. O'Brien and his eyes were a deep deep blue. And he didn't look like such a mean man.

I T WAS EARLY. The blue before day. And Colleen was outside gathering eggs. The wind whipped her hair in her face, tumbled her dress about. She knew now it did matter about the lost strongbox. The wagon man knew it was gone. Well, she would find that box and return it to that man. Secretly.

Ma's wind chimes sounded muted tones, and Colleen looked up. She had to get back, and she started walking to the cabin. It was time for breakfast.

Inside Cinder stood by the baby trying to lick her face. And Colleen ran quickly and stooped down to stroke the dog's head.

"Hey, Bonnie," Colleen said softly. She smiled at Bonnie, and Bonnie's little round face lit up. Her blue eyes shone, and she blinked.

Bonnie was theirs.

And she was going to make sure it stayed that way. And when she added wood to the stove for Ma, and hurried through half her chores before breakfast, she felt hopeful. It was going to work out.

Ma knew how she loved the river. Ma would let her go after breakfast, after chores, to the river. She'd take Shine, ride Shine to the river. But on the way she would look for the box. She would *find* the box.

Colleen ran to sit down at the table. "May I go to the river? After chores?"

Ma helped hominy onto Colleen and Jeb's plates. "Please, Ma, can I?" Ma stopped and looked at Colleen.

"And the mail stage is due," Colleen continued. "I could check for mail too."

News from Pennsylvania was always welcome. Ma nodded.

"After chores," she said.

Colleen was quiet then and ate her breakfast. Ma wondered about the wagon man. Did he say if he was settling in these parts, she asked Pa. Pa thought a second. "He didn't say. He asked about the Stockdale place. I told him Stockdale left Paul Russert in charge of it. There was some talk about a buyer from back east. Russert'll need to hire someone on to fix it up. The man, O'Brien, he seemed interested in that."

Colleen looked up. She stopped chewing. That wasn't it. Mary Kathleen had said they were going further west. That man just wanted to stay around and get that money-box back. And the baby's watch too, though he hadn't mentioned that yet. Maybe he didn't realize it was gone.

• • •

Colleen rode Shine, crisscrossing between the breaks, bearing south toward the river. "That box," Colleen told Shine. "It's out here somewhere." She looked back toward home, squinting in the sun. The cabin sat tiny in the grass. She couldn't see Jeb running about so she jumped off the horse.

When Shine bolted that night, he had run home, parallel to the breaks. North. She was sure. So the box was between the creek at home and the next one over. A mile, maybe more, away. Colleen looked that way. It was a lot of ground. But if she didn't find it today, she could come back every day or so. She would look every time she went for mail. She'd find the box sooner or later. She had to.

She led Shine, and Cinder ran ahead, his black form disappearing into a shining stand of switchgrass.

To the south a small, dark thing appeared, moving steadily across the land. Colleen kept her eye on it. A rider. He was making his way closer.

The wind swept the prairie, and shifted the colors of the grasses. Colleen stood still, listened. A meadowlark. The rush of wind in grass. Twice something dark caught her eye and she dropped the reins and ran to see. A pheasant's nest tucked beneath the folds of waving grass.

And then, stooped in a small draw, Colleen parted the grass and found not the metal box she searched for, but old buffalo bones in a tiny streambed, dry to the touch now, in the August heat.

Cinder was barking, and then Colleen heard hooves thundering, and she realized the rider was near. She stood. A black horse was running toward her, and would trample her, she thought. She tried to wave the horse and rider away, but they kept coming. Then Colleen backed up, tripped, fell to the ground, and she heard the heavy soft sound of hooves in grass coming to a stop.

The horse blew and whinnied loudly, and Colleen righted herself. Shine stood quietly with his reins hanging loose. Colleen grabbed her straw hat, put it on, and glared at the rider. Clay O'Brien. Mary Kathleen's husband. He knew she was here. He'd seen her horse.

His horse, a large black mare, twirled and pawed the ground. "Well . . . so it's the McCall girl," Clay O'Brien said, smiling.

Colleen could not see the deep blue of his eyes under the shade of his hat.

"And what might you be doing out here in the middle of nowhere . . . jumping out of the grass like a ground squirrel?"

Colleen squinted at the man. "You could have run me over! You could have killed me!" she said suddenly.

Her eyes flashed, and the steady wind drew her hair out from under her hat, flipped it about her face. She pushed it out of the way.

"If it's run you over I'd meant to do, you wouldn't be standing on those two bare feet," he told her.

The black mare tossed her head, and the man reined her back. He was staring curiously at Colleen. He was a nice-looking man, Colleen thought. She squinted at him. Sad eyes. A strong jaw. She began to fidget with her fingernails, still watching him.

In time he spoke again. "Do you have something you'd like to tell me?"

Colleen stared at him. "What?"

"You know. About you at the wagon . . . the night my wife died?"

"I don't know what you mean. . . ."

She did. She did know what he meant. The big mare thrust her head forward. Colleen stepped backward.

"Maybe now you remember something else, now your folks aren't around . . ."

Colleen opened her mouth, started to talk, but she stopped. A sullen look crossed her face. He was talking about the things she took. The strongbox, the watch.

Not Bonnie.

Colleen shook her head.

"You sure?"

She better say something. For Bonnie, she better. "No . . ." she said. "I don't remember anything else. Your wife, she was so sick. I couldn't make sense of half of what she said . . ."

"Is that so?"

Colleen frowned and nodded.

The man took his hat off, wiped his brow with the sleeve of his shirt.

"What about some . . . items . . . you might have picked up?"

"Stealing?" Colleen felt her heart beating in her neck. "I don't steal!"

"Stuff's gone. I been by that widow woman's. You and I know it weren't her."

"It wasn't me!" Her heart. It was pounding too hard. She couldn't say she *lost* the box. Then she'd have to explain why she *had* it. Even Ma and Pa wouldn't believe Mary Kathleen gave it to her for no reason.

They looked at each other, there in the bright summer sun, and neither said a word.

Purple wildflowers danced about under the black horse's nervous legs, and Colleen wished the man would go. Cinder scampered over and sat beside Colleen. His tongue hung out, and he looked at the man.

The O'Brien man seemed to have forgotten about Colleen. "Your dog?" he asked.

"My brother's."

"That little boy at the cabin?"

Colleen nodded. "Usually Cinder's with him. Night and day. But he came with me today."

For a time the man was quiet. "Had me a dog once," he finally said. "I wasn't no bigger than that boy . . . Was the first friend I ever had . . . last one too."

His eyes fixed on Cinder a moment longer, and Cinder stared back with his tongue lopping out.

The man waited a long time before speaking. "I'll be around," he said. "Russert needed somebody to ready that cabin, the outbuildings, for a buyer. So I'll be around . . ."

He turned the black horse then and was off.

Colleen watched him ride away. She watched the beautiful black horse and the quiet colors of the prairie's reaches.

That man, he must know she had the watch too. Bonnie's watch. But if she gave it back, if she gave all the things back, if she did that, surely the wagon man would go away. She could give the watch back, leave it over at the wagon in the grass where he'd find it.

No need to bother though without the box.

Colleen began walking again, searching the ground again. Occasionally she looked over her shoulder, squinting in the sun, toward the black horse and rider fading into the open spaces, into the greens and ambers.

"You'll kill that horse driving it that way," she muttered, and she watched the man and the horse sulkily for a minute before continuing her slow and divergent path to the river.

THE HOT SUN BURNED the top of Colleen's head, and the wind swept the grasslands from sky to sky. Colleen sat in the back of the buckboard, her knees up under her chin, and the wagon crawled along the ridge top.

It had been two months since the preacher had come to the settlement, but in mid-August, he came. They had gone to the service held in the dining room down at the hotel. They had taken Cinder to wait in the wagon during church. Ma had even packed a picnic lunch for them to eat so they would have time to visit. People from miles around came. Not many had seen Bonnie, and they all wanted to.

Colleen hated for the visiting to end, but now they had started home. She sat in the wagon in her good dress and her shoes that pinched her feet, her eyes on the silvery heads of the little bluestem. She took the shoes off and crawled over to Jeb. He was smart. He had carried his shoes to town and put them on only when he got to the steps of the hotel.

Jeb started expounding on the sermon the preacher had given.

"All liars go to hell."

"I'm glad you were listening," Ma called back to him.

Colleen laughed at Jeb. "Maybe you'll be a preacher someday," she said.

"No! A blacksmith!" Jeb yelled. He smiled his impish grin at her.

"Don't know," Colleen said.

She squinted off at the far sky.

All liars go to hell.

Did that mean her lies? The lies she told?

They weren't the same kind, were they? She had always been an honest girl. *Always.* And this about Bonnie . . . that wasn't the same as real lying.

It was *not* the same. It wasn't. She wouldn't think about it.

"Look, Ma." Colleen pointed at blue asters in the grass. "Can I pick some and walk home?"

Ma looked back.

"I won't be too late," Colleen said.

"Me too!" Jeb said.

"Can I take him, Ma? I'll look after him."

"I know you will, Colleen," Ma said. "You mind your sister, Jeb. Just remember, Colleen, I need you to help me with supper."

"I'll remember. And we can go to the river, Ma?"

"Just don't you be late."

Colleen and Jeb jumped off the wagon.

"Where we going?" Jeb asked.

"To get those asters . . . and to the river down near where the creek ends . . . and to the cemetery . . ."

"Why?"

" 'Cause Mary Kathleen O'Brien is there, and I was the last person on this earth to see her alive."

"Oh."

They ran then, through the wild grasses up toward asters sprinkled on the side of the slope. Colleen picked some and ran the rest of the way to the ridge top. She could see the cemetery on the bluff from there.

"Come on, Jeb!" Colleen yelled.

At the top of the bluff, Colleen stopped. She stood there and watched the wide Missouri, the shifting sandbars at the bend. Nothing grew on those bars. The river scoured them every year. But in the fall, snow geese would cover them. Snow geese and Canada geese and blue geese. They would cover her wide river and the sandbars. She missed the wild geese.

Colleen had come twice since the burying, gone by the grave both times on her way to the river. Not that it gave her any comfort. Far from it. But, she told herself, no one else knew the little baby was there. That was her sister. And no one knew Mary Kathleen O'Brien. Except Colleen McCall. Colleen wanted someone to go. So she went. She left wildflowers there.

She went over to Mary Kathleen's grave. Jeb had caught up by then, and he followed her. Colleen stooped down and put some of the asters there. Behind them, in the distance, the little river town baked in the hot August wind.

"Was she a nice lady?" Jeb asked.

Colleen stood up. "She was nice."

Jeb squinted at the flowers and the cross. "Were you scared?"

Colleen nodded. "Yes."

"Was that wagon woman scared?"

"She didn't seem like it," Colleen said. She looked over at Jeb.

They called to Cinder and followed the edge of the bluff heading to where the ravine would meet the river.

There were islands in the river. And a twisted trail going down to the flood plain across terraces left behind by a flood years gone. Colleen and Jeb liked that trail, liked the way it wound itself through young slender trees and shrubs, liked the way roots and earth formed steps as it curled its way lower toward the river. They ran and jumped and Cinder scrambled after them until the foot trail ended, and then past stands of young cottonwoods and peach-leaved willows they saw the edge of the river.

Colleen found a piece of driftwood to play fetch with Cinder. She tossed it as far as she could out into the water. Cinder loved it. He jumped up and down. He made happy little yelps. He brought back the driftwood over and over, and he shook water onto the children. Colleen turned her face and laughed.

"Let's get *our* hair wet," Jeb said. He ran to the water, bent over, his hands and feet in the water, and stuck his hair in. Colleen stared at him one moment. She knew what was coming next so she ran off laughing. Jeb shook his head like Cinder, and Cinder jumped up and down.

"We better let Cinder rest," Colleen said, walking back cautiously. "He might not know when he's had enough."

Jeb considered Cinder.

"Let's just put the stick down for now," Colleen told him, and they went to stand in the edge of the muddy river.

"Let's go out to them islands, Colleen," Jeb said.

Colleen smiled. "And come home with mud on our church clothes? Ma wouldn't like that."

Jeb and Colleen put their hands up to shield the sun and squinted out at the islands. Colleen looked down the river. She felt like running. "Race you!" she yelled back to Jeb.

She let Jeb catch up to her, and they raced along by the river with Cinder out ahead. And finally Colleen had to sit down on a log to catch her breath. She looked far across the shining river. Things were beginning to feel right again.

She would come back soon. In just a few weeks. The terns and plovers would be there, feeding on the mud flats, nesting on the sandbars. She would bring Jeb. He would like to see them, too.

They started home. Colleen took one last look back at the river.

The wagon man would go away, she told herself. He will wait awhile. But he will not know who has the box. He will give up and go away.

Colleen felt sure of it.

And that talk about hell. Surely the Lord would not send her to hell.

LATE AUGUST BROUGHT the terns to the sky. Plovers too. The choke cherries and wild plums ripened.

Pa came in near twilight every night. For days he'd been battling Russian thistle, keeping it down so it wouldn't get in the corn, so it wouldn't smother the hay.

"You tired, Pa?" Jeb said. He sprawled on his back on the floor.

"Yes, boy, it's a tiresome job."

"I'm tired too," Jeb said, rolling over on his stomach.

"Bonnie's awake, Pa," Colleen said, stooping near the baby's cradle. Cinder scratched his ear with his hind foot. "Bonnie says she wants to see you," Colleen said.

"And since when did our little Bonnie start talking?"

"Today . . ." Colleen laughed.

"And in full sentences, too," Pa mused. Pa went to Bonnie's cradle and picked Bonnie up. "Let's see this baby Bonnie," he said.

"Ah?" Bonnie said and she yawned. Colleen stood up beside Pa.

"What's that you say, Bonnie?" Pa asked, a smile in his eyes. "You're tired, too? You've been sweeping? Aren't you too little for that?" Bonnie gurgled and waved her arms. Pa put his ear to Bonnie's face. "Oh, you use a very little broom."

"Oh, Pa," Colleen said. She and Jeb laughed. Pa put Bonnie back down and went on to the table. He sat down slowly.

It had been some tiresome days all right, Colleen thought. Working in the garden. Hot winds. And a big garden. Almost an acre.

So Colleen was thrilled when Ma told her at supper she had an errand for her to run tomorrow afternoon. Thrilled until she heard more.

"Hannah Jones has been wanting to borrow the candle molds. I want you to carry them over there," Ma told her.

The widow? Colleen would just as soon not see the widow.

But after supper Ma put the candle molds in a canvas bag and wrote a little note to the widow. Colleen watched her mother with a small frown.

The next day Colleen took Shine, and on her way to the widow's, she roamed the prairie east of the ravine as was her habit now, keeping to the open prairie between the breaks, her eyes down, searching for the metal box.

In time, though, Colleen came to a small ravine further east, and stopped. The cottonwoods would be turning yellow before long.

She squinted in the sun and watched some coyote pups running around. They were playing with a piece of driftwood. Colleen smiled. Tug of war, she thought. She saw no sign of the mother.

The pups ran off in a bit. Colleen followed them with her eyes till they disappeared. She'd hear them sometimes at night. Grown coyotes. Somewhere farther out on the prairie. Somewhere upstream.

Never mind about that box, she told herself. The wagon man, Mr. O'Brien, he had not been back. The last she'd seen of him was early August. Now August would be gone in another week. They had little Bonnie. Ma and Pa and her, they would take care of Bonnie.

The sky churned with slow slate-gray and white clouds against a glowing blue sky, and Colleen wondered if there might be a storm coming.

She rode south until she pulled the horse to a stop again, this time squinting at the widow's cabin in the distance and the widow's sons' cabins even further away, only tiny smidgens in the yellows and greens of the prairie.

There was a hint of a wagon path there in the grass.

Colleen guided Shine that way, and soon she saw the widow standing outside of her log house, and it seemed to Colleen that the widow was watching, waiting.

She stared at the dark figure, the dark dress moving in the endless wind, and somewhere deep inside Colleen wanted to leave right then. But she gripped the reins and the horse walked slowly on.

MA SENT THE CANDLE molds for you . . . ," Colleen said. She jumped down from the horse and began to untie the bag from the saddle. The widow wouldn't think she was polite if she just handed the candle molds to her from the horse. So, standing on the ground, Colleen untied the canvas bag from Ma and then fumbled in her pinafore, finding the note Ma had sent along, and she held out the note and the bag for the widow.

"Thank you, Colleen," Widow Jones said. Colleen smiled and nodded.

"How is your mother?" the widow asked her.

"She's well," Colleen said.

"She should be eating organ meat, you know, to get her blood built back up."

"Yes, ma'am. I'll tell her."

"Any news from your folks in Pennsylvania?" One of the widow's sons, the one back east, had been wounded at Fredericksburg. And the widow tried to keep up.

"Not lately. No, ma'am, but if we hear anything . . . about the war . . . I know Ma'll want to let you know."

"Tell her I do appreciate that." The widow paused. "And the baby?"

Colleen's eyes shone. "Bonnie, she's wonderful!" She laughed. "She watches us now when we pick her up and . . . and she loves to chew on her hand!"

A round log barn sat in the distance. Colleen looked back and forth at it and then the widow, and she remembered Ma always said that she was rude to let her eyes wander when speaking to someone. So Colleen tried again to keep her eyes on the widow's.

"It's so sad about the other little soul . . . and that poor woman."

Colleen swallowed and glanced to the far rim of the prairie and then back at the widow. She twisted at the loose ties on her pinafore but kept her eyes on the widow's.

"The husband was by here the other day. You know, Paul Russert's hired him to fix up the Stockdale place for a buyer from back east."

Colleen looked hard at Widow Jones. "The woman in the wagon's husband?" Colleen asked though she knew that's who the widow was talking about. The widow nodded, and Colleen frowned. What did the wagon man say to the widow? What did the widow say?

"Did the mother tell you what she wanted to name her baby? For a marker. When I spoke to the husband, Mr. O'Brien, the other day, I told him he should ask you if she said anything about a name."

Name? Colleen's eyes flashed down to the ties in her hands and back up to the widow. She tried to remember. Did Mary Kathleen O'Brien say anything about a name?

A bird called nearby. Clear. Colleen knitted her brows together, and looked over toward the widow's barn hoping to see the bird.

"Name. I don't think so . . . It's hard to remember all she said. I try, but . . ."

"Colleen . . ."

Colleen looked back. "Yes, ma'am?"

"Mr. O'Brien said that you told him the baby was already dead when you got there that night."

Already dead. Already dead.

Colleen's head swirled inside. Yes. That was what she had told him. But she did not remember what she had told the widow that night. *Please, Lord,* she began to pray, *don't let me say something wrong.* She nodded her head.

"You told me the baby was alive when you got there."

Colleen's heart picked up its beat. Too fast. Her heart was going too fast. And it seemed hard to breathe. She stared at the widow and the endless wind blew Colleen's hair across her face and blew the widow's black-green dress about. And a whirl of birds swept by in the oncoming sunset.

Say something, Colleen insisted to herself inside her head.

"I . . . everything happened so fast, Widow Jones . . . What I said . . . I thought it was alive . . . but I got to thinking it probably wasn't. At first I thought it was, I thought it was asleep. . . ."

Suddenly Colleen shut her mouth. She backed up to the horse and her eyes flashed at the widow. Dark clouds were collecting on the horizon.

It's our baby now, she screamed inside. She knows us. She coos when we hold her. Mary Kathleen O'Brien gave her to me.

She grabbed for Shine's reins while she watched the widow. Look at her, she told herself. It's rude not to look at her.

So Colleen held the widow's gaze, and the widow studied her, and the wind rushed by Colleen's ears. It was cooler now than earlier. It was getting late.

"It was a hard night for all of you," the widow said finally.

"I have to go now," Colleen said breathlessly. "Ma'll be waiting." She stood for a moment and the widow watched her. Colleen turned quickly then and climbed on the horse. You should wish people a good evening, Ma always told her. "I hope you have a nice evening," Colleen told the widow. And she looked at the widow a moment longer before riding off.

"She doesn't know *anything*," she muttered to Shine. "No one knows anything."

Colleen rode west. She would follow the trail by the ravine to Mary Kathleen O'Brien's wagon, and then home. Shrubs speckled the landscape as she neared the break.

She could see the creek at the bottom of the slope.

Why did the widow have to be so particular? How could she remember every word said that night? Colleen didn't even remember herself.

In minutes it would be dark. A mink scampered between trees on the other side. Colleen breathed easier and smiled at the dark little form. She wouldn't waste her time fretting over that old Widow Jones anymore.

Colleen and Shine followed the foot trail toward home. She watched for the wagon, wondering had Mr. O'Brien moved it, or would it still be right where she first saw it shining so bright in the sun?

It was there. Still there near the ravine.

"Whoa, Shine . . ."

Colleen looked for the man. No one was around. Some distance off near the barn she saw a swaybacked gray horse, dappled. A pretty color. But no sign of Clay O'Brien.

She looked back to the wagon and the grasses around it glowed darkly in the twilight's deep blues. The wagon seemed a ghost wagon blending to shades of indigo. A ghost wagon almost fading to nothing.

She wished she could have known Mary Kathleen O'Brien. She knew she would have liked her. Someday she would give Bonnie the beautiful watch. Someday she would tell her about Mary Kathleen O'Brien.

Far off a bell was sounding. She recognized it as Ma's cowbell on the ridgepole. Ma fussed when she was late.

"Come on, Shine," she said. "Let's go home." Yet in her heart she wished she did not have to leave that wagon there lost in the wind. All alone under that giant dimming sky.

COLLEEN HAD NOT BEEN to the grave since the middle of August. When she went with Jeb. Yet the ghost wagon lingered in her dreams, and she took it in her mind to go. She asked Ma if she could ride Shine to the river, and she promised to be back before sunset.

Ma said she could go to the river if she liked, but to take something warm, a wrap of some kind, September evenings bringing a new coolness to the air. So Colleen put on last year's woolen dress. But with frost probably at least a month away, Colleen decided she still needed no shoes.

She stood on the bluff at the edge of the cemetery, her bare feet on the cool grass, and watched the river, low and wide and choppy.

She needed to hurry. Ma would do more than scold her for being late this time. Ma was tired of Colleen's incessant tardiness, and Colleen had dawdled today, collecting the asters she now held in her hand, leading Shine this way and that, drifting in an ambling path across the prairie. But she could not tell Ma that.

Colleen would leave the asters on the grave. It would

not be right to hurry. She looked down at the wildflowers and squeezed her fingers around them. Beautiful asters. Colleen held back her shoulders then and walked slowly, determinedly, to the grave, and she knew it was late, but she did not run. She placed the blue flowers there, the blue petals now part of the grave.

"I hope you're not mad I haven't been by here lately," Colleen said, "but I figure maybe you're not here anymore anyhow . . . being a spirit now . . ."

Colleen looked over her shoulder. There was no one there, but Colleen hushed her voice anyway. "I met him, Mary Kathleen. I met your husband."

The wind rose a little, and some stray leaves from river trees tumbled and stopped by her feet. The grass stirred.

"He thinks I stole those things you gave me . . . but I guess naturally he would," she whispered now. "And I'm confused. And don't be mad . . . but . . ."

Colleen remembered the man's eyes resting on Cinder. He had had a dog. A dog that was his friend when he was a little boy. Like Jeb.

"He doesn't seem like such a bad sort. . . . " Colleen stared at the grave. She started to walk away but turned back.

"Even so . . . I believe you, Mary Kathleen. . . . I'll keep my promise . . ."

She would have run to Shine then. Except something

farther down on the edge of the bluff, west of the tiny cemetery caught her eye. And Colleen stood still, standing by the grave, watching.

There on the bluff she saw a man. A small figure fifty yards off, standing dark against the flaming sky of the setting sun. Wild black grasses bent there in the wind, and the man's long coat rolled around his legs.

She knew who that man was.

And she was sure he was watching her. She stood there and stared back at him.

A dangerous man, Mary Kathleen had told her. There were more words. More of Mary Kathleen's words. She searched for them in her mind but could not find them.

Last year, when they had the Indian scare, after they came back from Yankton, Pa had given Ma a knife to carry in her apron pocket when he was on patrol. A knife that stayed in a leather sheath. Ma didn't carry it anymore now but Colleen knew where it stayed.

She would find it, and take it for her own.

The hair on her arms tingled, and she wanted to look away. But she held the dark man's gaze so that he would know she saw him. He wanted her to see him. She did. He wanted her to be afraid. He would not see her fear. She made up her mind to that.

But Colleen was afraid.

She took one last look and made herself turn away,

her face again to the grave and the flowers she had put there, and she began to walk toward the horse. And she did not look back then. Only when she reached the spot where she left Shine, when she was almost to Shine, did she look. And he was gone.

Colleen rode away toward home remembering the man in the dark wind, and the secret she held in her heart.

When Colleen was near home, she heard the supper bell ringing on the wind, and she realized she was late and would have to explain now why she had dawdled so, and she knew she would lie.

J EB AND CINDER WERE running about between the cabin and the barn, dark little forms, a shadow boy and his dog. Jeb ran yelling to the cabin when he spotted Colleen and disappeared into the open door. Colleen hurried to bed Shine down and ran to the cabin.

Inside, the candles were lit. Pa looked up at Colleen from the table. Ma glanced at her from the stove. And Jeb eyed her sideways from where he stood, dead in his tracks on his way across the room.

Colleen took a breath. Jeb looked to Pa and back to her.

"I stopped along the creek," Colleen said, hesitating, looking over at Ma and back to Pa, and all Colleen could hear was the spoon hitting the pan as Ma stirred the hominy.

"I saw a raccoon . . . ," she added. She bit her bottom lip. She watched her pa. And she waited.

Ma looked up at her and then back at Pa.

"I'm sorry . . . about being late . . ."

"I can't understand, Colleen," Ma said. "A girl so careful watching out for Jeb and the baby. You never need reminding to do chores." Ma looked back at the hominy pot.

"Your ma worries, Colleen," Pa told her.

Colleen was told she would not be stepping one foot off the half section for a week.

In the candlelight Colleen slumped at the wooden table picking at her supper. Listening. The talk shifted to the war back east. The army of the Potomac, General Grant. Lee. Gettysburg falling. People they knew back in Pennsylvania. Ma told Colleen to sit up and eat.

Jeb had seen a Union cap over near the ravine close to the Stockdale place that afternoon. Pa had taken him along to get some kindling in the breaks.

Colleen looked up. What if Jeb went over there by himself? Over near where the man was. Colleen's eyes darted between Ma and Pa.

Jeb had seen the cap in a small pile of rubbish, near the top of the break, like it was waiting to be burned.

Colleen put down her fork. "He better not go over there by himself, Pa," Colleen said. "Tell him he can't go. Please."

Pa looked at Colleen.

"And I seen a Springfield . . . leaning up on that big old wagon," Jeb continued. "Where'd that man get that cap, Pa?"

"Mr. O'Brien's his name," Colleen said to Jeb. She gave a hurried look to Ma, to Pa. "Maybe he's a deserter," she said.

He could be, it seemed to her. Maybe.

Ma gave both children a stern look. "Springfields. Six years old and talks like he's in the militia," Ma said. She looked at Pa and she shook her head. "And you, Colleen. Where on earth do you come up with such ideas?"

"I'm almost seven, Ma," Jeb said.

"Both of you just hush and eat your supper," Ma said.

More of Mary Kathleen O'Brien's words tried to surface. Words Colleen had paid little mind to on that dark night. Something Mary Kathleen said, about her husband coming out here to the Dakota Territory. About federal marshals. About so much territory to cover out here. "Maybe he lied," Colleen said suddenly. "Maybe he's one of those bounty jumpers or maybe he . . ."

Ma gave Colleen a long look. Colleen took a bite of hominy and shut her mouth and began to chew. What was she doing? The least she said about Mr. O'Brien the better. She would never talk anymore about him. Never.

She better watch out for Jeb though, Colleen thought. Watch him herself. Keep track of him. Jeb was *her* responsibility. After all, *she* was the one who decided not to tell anyone what the wagon woman said.

I T WAS MORE THAN a week into September. Golden
sun warmed the prairie. And milkweed was burst-
ing open. Colleen and Jeb, their fingers to the sun,
chased the silky seed puffs that quietly danced above the
grasses just out of their reach. Colleen soon stopped and
bent over, her hands on her knees, laughing. "You'll
never catch it," she shouted to Jeb.

She watched Jeb and Cinder a moment, and then
turned and ran back along the top of the ridge. She had
Bonnie there in her basket. "I came right back," she told
Bonnie, dropping to the ground. "But Jeb and Cinder
have left us for good!"

Bonnie kicked happily, and Colleen tickled her a moment. She got back to her feet and took Bonnie in her
arms.

From the ridge she could see the Stockdale place, the
cabin and barn no longer hidden by grasses or the lay of
the land. The roofs had been repaired. She narrowed her
eyes studying it.

"Beautiful dreamer, wake unto me . . . ," Colleen sang

to Bonnie. She shifted from foot to foot and swayed back and forth, continuing to gaze south.

"Starlight and dewdrops are waiting for thee . . ."

"Colleen!" Ma called.

"He's most done, that man. He's most done mending that place up," Colleen whispered. "He'll probably go off some other place any time now. A month from now . . . probably . . . by the time the geese come."

"Colleen!"

"Ma's calling us," Colleen said, still looking toward the Stockdale place, before grabbing the basket and hurrying back.

Inside Colleen put Bonnie in her cradle. She lingered there, her face over Bonnie's, and Bonnie watched her intently. Colleen whispered, "By the time the geese come . . ." She put her finger to her lips and touched Bonnie's nose. She'd been a good baby from the first.

Ma set Colleen to churning cow butter, and began tending to Bonnie. Outside the prairie wind sighed in the slender grasses, and Colleen heard the cowbell jangle on the ridgepole.

"Tomorrow you can help me work with Jeb on his letters," Ma said. "It's time we get back to your lessons, too. And I think we'll have time to clean and refill the straw ticks on all the beds."

Colleen turned suddenly at that, and then hid her surprise by focusing intently on the churn. She glanced toward her own bed.

Dear Kind Stranger . . .

Why hadn't she destroyed that letter? Mary Kathleen's letter!

She stopped churning and hugged her elbows tightly, and she did not notice Ma was watching her closely.

"Is something wrong, Colleen?"

Colleen looked up quickly at her ma, her expression blank. "No, ma'am," she said. "Everything's fine." And Colleen began churning again.

Colleen decided she would tear the letter into a hundred pieces and bury it down near the creek. At twilight she told Ma she was going to the ravine.

But Ma said no. "Storm's coming, Colleen. You stay near the cabin."

So Colleen straggled about between the cabin and the barn, wondering where else she might hide that letter.

She folded her arms and scratched the back of her ankle with her other bare foot. She watched Jeb and Cinder digging in the dirt around the side of the cabin.

In Jeb's hand was a small tin cup Pa had given him for making forts in the dirt. Jeb and Cinder were intent on whatever they were doing. Colleen glanced at the barn.

Ma was busy in the cabin. Ma never went to the barn at twilight. And Pa. Pa had left to search for a stray. Colleen dashed back in the cabin for the lantern and scampered off to the barn.

It was dark inside. The warm smell of hay laced with the scent of manure hung in the air. Colleen stopped in the doorway and looked quickly toward the cabin. Flashes of lightning glimmered in the far sky. She looked out to the north toward the neighbors. The Newmans' place blurred into the dark reaches of the land. But a half mile off at the Russerts', she saw the tiniest of lights. Pa had headed that way. He'd be back soon. She'd best hurry.

Colleen went to Shine's stall and rubbed his face and he nickered. The hoe hung on the wall. She would need to loosen the hard earth in the corner of the barn. . . . And so, kneeling down, Colleen set the lantern on top of her old trunk.

She scraped the straw away, first with the heavy pitchfork and then with her hands. She chopped at the dirt floor with the hoe. The ground was too hard. She glanced to the door.

A little hole would do for now. And she would move her trunk over on top of it. Stooping down, she felt the dry, newly-tilled earth with her finger, and she pulled the letter out of the pocket in her pinafore and squeezed it in her hand.

The tiny flame from the lantern warmed the dark colors in the barn, and the animals stirred in their stalls. Colleen's eyes darted about following the quivering light. In the corner, an old sickle bar shone dully. Colleen glanced again to the door.

Colleen ripped the letter into tiny pieces, pushing them in the hole.

"What're you doin'?"

Colleen looked up. Jeb was standing there beside her.

COLLEEN SCRAMBLED TO her feet and glared at
Jeb. At the same time, her elbow toppled the
lantern off the trunk to the floor, and Colleen turned
and stared at it. It lay near the straw.

Then the smell of smoke. A small clump of hay burst
into flame. Colleen grabbed the lantern and rolled it to
the cleared ground.

"The tarp," she shouted at Jeb. He stared at her so she
scrambled herself to grab a small piece of tarpaulin behind her trunk and smothered the bright sparks with it.
It was easy, but Colleen was shaken and she scrambled to
her knees, her breath coming in fast, deep tracks.

She looked around. The lantern still had light.

"It's all right," she told Jeb.

Swallowing hard, she picked the lantern up and settled it back on the trunk. The cinders, she smashed into
the ground with her hands. "See, it's all right," she said.

Over her shoulder, past Jeb, she saw the barn door.
There was no one there. Her eyes went back to the
singed straw. Part of Mary Kathleen's letter, still untorn,
lay by the barn wall.

"Don't you tell," Colleen said. She sat on her heels and tore the paper to bits, pushed it in the small hole and dragged the trunk on top of it. She stood up and ran to the door. It was almost dark outside now. There was no sign of Ma or Pa.

Colleen went back to Jeb and grabbed him by his shoulders, squeezing them. "You promise me you won't tell."

"I don't have to," Jeb said, shaking loose. He glared back at her.

Colleen sighed. She was quiet. "I'm sorry . . . ," she said. She bit off a hangnail and watched him hopefully. Thunder rumbled in the distance.

"You're mean," Jeb told her.

A flash of lightning, and a faint sound. The wind picking up outside, Colleen thought. A gust whished in the door. Colleen stooped down again. The palms of her hands smoothed across the cool straw to make sure no tinder was smoldering.

Jeb scurried over to the barn door, and Colleen blew out the flame in the lantern. She could see Jeb's dark little figure against the faint light from outside. She followed him, and they stood in the dark watching the lightning.

Colleen bit on her little fingernail. She couldn't let Jeb tell about the letter. She couldn't. Maybe if she told Jeb something, told him part of the truth.

"I will tell you a secret, but you will have to promise not to tell."

"I don't have to promise."

"I'm gonna tell you anyway," she said. Jeb looked at her.

"Remember I told you I met a woman the night Bonnie was born . . ."

"That woman that died?"

Colleen nodded. "That woman wanted me to take a gold watch for Ma's baby. It was a watch for the wagon woman's baby, and since her baby died, she wanted Ma's baby to have it . . ."

Jeb's eyes were big. "Why?" he asked.

"Because I had come by there and helped her. And it's a secret. That woman's husband might not have wanted her to give the watch away."

"Let me see it," Jeb demanded.

"If you're good, and if you do promise, then I'll show you."

"Why can't we tell?" Jeb wanted to know. "Let's tell Ma. She wouldn't tell . . ."

"If we tell . . . if we tell, Jeb . . . something terrible might happen."

"What?"

"I can't say now," Colleen said. "But I'll tell you when you're a little older."

Jeb put on a big frown. He did not like it.

"I will," Colleen promised. "Now what about you? Will you agree to keep this secret?"

Jeb pouted.

"And I'll show you what the woman gave me for little Bonnie."

"When?"

"Tomorrow . . ."

Jeb nodded his head slowly. "Well . . . all . . . right . . . ," he said. And he smiled.

Colleen smiled back, but inside her heart raced on.

The air smelled faintly of rain. "Come on," Colleen said. She ran out in the night air, and Jeb followed. They ran up to the small hill behind the barn where the grass was long and wild and tickled their legs and arms, and they waited, watching brilliant bolts streak the sky. And the whole prairie became alive with thin white light that trembled before darkness came.

Pa's small herd of cattle was moving toward the outbuildings. And they saw Pa was back and out that way on his horse.

Small raindrops hit their faces and arms, and the thunder tore through the night then, and they screamed and laughed and ran to stand under the eaves outside the barn.

Colleen feared for the blue lightning that Pa had seen once on the horns of cattle, but they did not see that, and Colleen said it was because the lightning wasn't close enough for that to happen. They watched the cattle become ghost cattle in the lightning that lit the miles and miles of sky.

Colleen saw Ma at the door of the cabin. Wind-driven raindrops scattered under the eaves. The storm was too close now. "We gotta get inside," Colleen said, and she ran to the cabin. Bonnie. Bonnie might be afraid. She'd better be there to see that did not happen.

She stopped inside the door and looked back once more. She saw the shapes of the cattle, black as the night against the brilliant sky on top of the ridge past the haystacks, and then the lightning was gone, and everything was black again. Pa was still out there. He would want to calm the cattle. Thunder, shaking the very air, rolled across the earth. Jeb was jumping up and down in the barnyard, but the thunder brought him running in, and Ma came and closed the door against the rain.

COLLEEN SAT ON THE little stoop beside the front door the next morning. Her chores were done. The air was chilled, but the sun was warming it. Twisting backward, she peered inside the cabin.

"Ma? May I help Jeb finish so we can go on to the creek?"

"You know your pa won't abide that. Jeb will do his own chores."

Colleen sighed. She had *promised*. She *had* to show him the watch today. Or else . . .

The horses grazed in the drifting wind, and above her a hawk wheeled in the sky. Colleen watched it soaring there. She watched it till it swept away.

Finally Jeb finished. The children ran past the chicken coop and into the wild grasses. They ran to the edge of the ravine where the footpath turned and twisted down toward the creek. Colleen put her hand on Jeb's arm, stopping him from heading down the path. She supposed there to be no one in the ravine. But she squinted, looking anyway. Willows and shrubs. Cottonwoods. The creek trailed silently along.

"I don't see nobody," Jeb said.

"Me neither," Colleen said, still looking.

"I bet I know where you hid it." Jeb grinned. "The best hiding place of all. Wanna know where? Wanna?"

"Where?"

"Down yonder." Jeb pointed down the creek. "Down where me 'n' Pa seen them rattlesnakes. You know the place. With that big old rock."

Colleen knew the place. More than once they had seen rattlers there.

"Did you hide it there?"

"No. No, that wouldn't be such a good place, Jeb. We wouldn't want to put it where there might be more snakes than here."

"But nobody'd ever want to look there. 'Cause uh the snakes. See?"

Colleen shook her head. "No, nobody but us knows about that. And there could be more snakes."

They followed the little path, and Colleen led Jeb down the creek to the place she had hidden the watch.

Jeb looked around over his shoulders and waited for his sister to show him the wonderful golden treasure she had come by.

Colleen got out the knife and used it to help break open the earth. About a foot down, she brought out the crockery, dusting off the clinging dirt and showed the little boy the beautiful watch.

Jeb took it in his hands. "Look at it, Colleen!" he said. "Real gold!" He looked up at Colleen, his eyes shining.

"Let me show you inside," Colleen said, taking the watch and popping it open. She handed it back.

"Ohhh!" Jeb said.

Colleen smiled, and showed him how to close it back, and Jeb held his arm out and let the watch swing on its chain.

"I wish we could show Ma and Pa," Jeb said, and he squinted at the watch and held it up over his head, and Colleen felt a wave of fear crawl over her.

She pressed her lips together and waited a moment. "We can't," she said quietly. Jeb was busy examining the watch. "We better put it back now," Colleen told him. She wrapped the watch quickly, her eyes darting about the ravine, and she pushed it back in the jar and buried it.

And as Colleen was pushing the soft earth down, as she was patting it and leaning on it, just then she heard something. A noise downstream that made her look that way. She stood and glanced up and down the sides of the ravine. She looked back at Jeb. He had heard it too. His brown eyes stared at Colleen.

"Hey!" she yelled.

Some small willows with thin, silver-white leaves shivered in a sudden gust of wind.

"Hey! Who's there?"

Still there was no answer.

"Come on!" She ran away and stooped behind a thick shrub. She heard it again. But now it sounded like some men cutting wood. Further down the creek, cutting wood. That was all. A good ways off, too.

So Colleen and Jeb went to the creek. Colleen rubbed her arms, though she wasn't really cold, and waded into the water. She knew the water would still be cold. It didn't matter. The sun warmed her. Jeb stooped at the edge, looking.

"A frog, Colleen!" Jeb yelled. "I almost got it!" He bent over the water, his squatty little hands outstretched. "Where'd it go?" He reached for a bright spot under the water. A dry, wavy cottonwood leaf trailed past them.

When Colleen turned she heard the shot. It rang out through the ravine, and she saw a man on horseback coming from downstream. The water splashed up from the horse's hooves. Splashed on the gray, black-dappled legs of a horse she had seen before. It was the horse she had seen near the Stockdale cabin. One of the wagon man's horses.

She moved in front of Jeb. "If I tell you to, you run and get Pa," she told Jeb.

C LAY O'BRIEN GOT down off the horse, rubbed his nose and looked to the top of the ravine. His rifle hung loose in the crook of his arm, and the barrel wavered carelessly toward the children.

"Mornin'," he said.

He waited, watching her. Colleen nodded.

The September sun cast sharp shadows from him and the horse to the earth.

Colleen felt her heart, heavy inside. Beating fast. "What were you shooting so close for?" she asked.

The man looked over to Jeb and back to Colleen.

"Close? You mean back there?" He shook his head. "Thought I saw a jackrabbit. You didn't hear a shot close by here. Echo's what you heard."

"I did! I know I did! There was a shot close to here," Colleen said.

She shut her mouth. He was lying to her. The shot had been close.

We should go, Colleen thought.

Clay O'Brien squinted at her from under the brim of his hat.

"Jeb!" Colleen said. "Come on!" Her eyes stayed on the man. She backed away. But Jeb did not move.

"Hold on a minute," Clay O'Brien said. "I don't want any trouble now."

"We have to go . . . back home," Colleen said to the man, trying to make her voice sound at ease. "We have chores. . . . Come on, Jeb." Jeb glanced at Colleen and back at the man.

Colleen waited. Jeb stooped back down by the water. He didn't understand. They needed to get out of there. Colleen moved to the water's edge and bent over him, cupped her hand to his ear. "Come on, Jeb! Now!" she whispered through gritted teeth into his ear. "And don't talk to him," she added. She straightened up and looked at the man.

The man was watching, an amused look on his face. And Colleen began to work her way backward again, edging up the slope. "Jeb!"

"Why?" Jeb whined, turning momentarily to glare at her. "That *frog's* here!"

Colleen tilted her head to the side and glared back. "We have to go, Jeb."

"Now . . . I'll only be a minute," Clay O'Brien said. His manner was easygoing, almost friendly. "You . . ." He looked squarely at Colleen. "You need to tell me where that box is . . . and the watch."

"She don't have a box, mister," Jeb said.

Clay O'Brien smiled at that, but his eyes stayed on Colleen. "You don't want your pa to know what you done. . . . You get smart, and this thing'll be over 'n' done with."

"You got a pretty horse," Jeb said suddenly. "I never seen one of those."

The horse was the Appaloosa, the one Colleen had seen before. It looked tired and old.

"That good for nothing old nag. Half dead." O'Brien chuckled.

Jeb frowned at him.

"I don't need to be telling you again, McCall girl, do I?"

Colleen didn't know how to answer that. She wanted to go. But Jeb wouldn't do right. Maybe the man would go.

The O'Brien man turned and put his hand on the horse's neck. But he did not leave. He looked up the creek bank. Cottonwoods shimmered there, startling yellow against the blue September sky. And he squinted again at Colleen.

"Why were you watching me at the river last week?" Colleen said suddenly. "At the cemetery?"

O'Brien chuckled and scratched the hair behind his ear and continued to watch her silently.

"Why?!"

O'Brien grinned. "You know why," he said slowly. Quietly. "Don't you?"

"I do not."

O'Brien looked to his side down the ravine, looked up at the brilliant sky, looked back at Colleen.

"There I was," he said, "on my way back from Chouteau Creek, and I stop there on the river bluff. Take a long look. 'That's a strange one,' I said to myself. 'What's that girl spooking around this here grave place for? Why's she haunting my poor wife's grave?' "

Colleen stood still, her eyes fixed on the man's. She could see the old horse behind him lowering its head.

"There are people I know been buried there."

"There you were, and it wasn't the first time you been there. There at Kathleen O'Brien's grave . . . my wife . . . you . . . and you didn't know my wife. . . ." O'Brien rubbed his forefinger across his chin. "What to make of that?"

Colleen stared at him.

"No answer?" The man seemed to be weighing her lack of an answer in his mind.

He shook his head, and grasped the saddle horn. "It's a shame," he mused. "A shame for Kathleen. You people got no fitter place to bury someone 'cept'n the same place you bury 'breeds?" He chuckled like he had said something funny.

Colleen narrowed her eyes. It was a mean thing to say. A cruel thing. "That's not funny," Colleen said.

There was a little grave. A little grave there at the cemetery. Ma had shown it to her one time. It was a little girl's grave. A little girl with an Indian mother and a white father. Half-breed. That was what that awful man meant.

The man got back up in the saddle and turned the horse abruptly. Splashes from the horse's sudden movements sprinkled the children, and the man headed the horse back downstream.

"We can't tell Pa and Ma about this," Colleen whispered, her tone serious. She and Jeb were quiet. They stood there and watched. "That's a mean man," Colleen said out loud. "You mustn't ever talk to him anymore. You should have come with me when I said."

They ran back up out of the ravine all the way to the cabin. Colleen made corn and milk for the chickens and fed them, and after that she helped Ma bathe Bonnie.

Colleen couldn't help wondering why Clay O'Brien, if he was so sure she had his things, why didn't he say that to Pa? Or why didn't he get the law?

That afternoon Colleen helped Ma draw wicks in the tubes of the candle molds, and words Mary Kathleen O'Brien had said played in her mind. Words about the money in the strongbox . . . ill gotten . . . the war back east.

Now she remembered! The man had come back from the war and he had the money and it wasn't right.

The O'Brien man must not want the law involved.

Colleen figured it was a good thing for her, too, he wasn't getting the law. There was a hanging judge up at Chouteau Creek Station, and Colleen guessed that judge didn't hang children, but the idea worried her anyhow. People were afraid of that judge up the Missouri . . .

COLLEEN LOOKED AND looked for the box. When she went for mail. When she had time to play and ride Shine. She did not know where exactly Shine ran that night. And she did not know where the box fell off the horse. So she looked everywhere. She could not find it. But still she looked.

Early one morning Mr. Russert came by and talked to Pa. Clay O'Brien was leaving. He was most done with the work Mr. Russert had hired him to do. He still had some new ground to break, the corral to mend. But sometime before the first freeze he'd be leaving for points west.

Early in the afternoon Colleen and Jeb dug potatoes and turnips, and Colleen almost didn't mind digging in the dirt. Not now that the O'Brien man was leaving. She sat back on her heels and looked out to the skyline. Maybe there were geese at the river. She would go look this afternoon. She smiled just thinking about it.

She couldn't help but wonder though why Clay O'Brien was leaving without the things he thought she stole. He might have given up. That might be it. He had no proof. Still she would look for the box this afternoon. Just in case. After all, she wouldn't want him coming over and asking Pa for it now. Colleen's good spirits were dampened at that thought, but there was time before it got cold, she thought, and she made up her mind to find the man's box before then.

When the garden was done, Colleen saddled Shine and led him out in the sun. Jeb came running and hollering. "Me too!" he yelled, and he stopped beside her, smiling.

Colleen smiled back at him.

"I want to ride Shine," Jeb announced. "You ride Bayboy."

"You know Pa doesn't want you on Shine. He's too spirited. Besides, you can't go this time . . . I've got Shine ready to go to the river. I'm leaving now." Colleen turned to tighten the girth on the horse.

"Me too. You promised I could go, too . . ."

Colleen paused and looked at him. It was true. She had promised she would take him the next time she went.

"Oh! Oh, Jeb, I'm sorry . . . I forgot. But I'll take you next time."

Jeb scowled at her. "You said I could go this time."

Colleen got up in the saddle. She looked down at Jeb. She did promise, but she was going to look for that box. It would take too long to saddle another horse and take him, too.

"It can't be today, Jeb. I'm sorry. Really . . ."

"It's supposed to be today!" Jeb yelled.

Colleen looked at him. She hated being this way. She squinted at him and bit her bottom lip. She did not want to tell him no. She had to tell him no. "Next time," she said, and she turned the horse quickly.

She left for the river without him.

"I hate you!" Jeb shouted.

There were no geese at the river, and Colleen's trip was ruined by her broken promise to Jeb. An autumn coolness covered the whole prairie. The new slant of the mid-September sun colored everything in a bright, low light. Colleen made herself search for the box longer than she wanted to, riding back and forth, further east than she had looked before, close to a shallow ravine there. So as not to waste the trip entirely. She looked for geese, too, on her way home, but saw nothing more than a wide and lonely sky.

She wondered if Jeb was still mad at home. She wished she had brought him along.

When she got back, the sun was low. Pa still was not back from hunting so supper would be later than usual. Colleen found Jeb in back of the barn, out of the wind, drawing in the dirt with half of an old flail. She stood watching him scratch on the ground.

"Jeb . . ."

No answer.

Colleen stepped closer. "Are you still mad at me? I am sorry. I wish I wasn't so mean."

Jeb shot a glance at Colleen before looking back at the ground and his drawings. He threw the flail down, crawled under the fence into the corral and sat on the ground drawing with his fingers.

"I am sorry, really," Colleen said, taking a step forward.

Jeb squinted at his hand, tracing around it with his finger in the dirt. He would not look at Colleen.

IN THE MORNING JEB carried the washboard for Ma to the creek. He righted the large ten-gallon kettle from where it was lodged between two willows, too. Ma brought the dirty laundry, and Colleen carried little Bonnie, and a basket for her to sleep in while Colleen helped Ma with the washing.

Jeb waded in the edge of the creek, and squatted down studying the water for anything alive. Before long he got a stick and began dragging it in the water.

Colleen struggled to wring out a freshly washed shirt. "Jeb . . . ," she warned.

Jeb took the stick and sliced it through the air, making a soft whizzing sound. It slung tiny drops of creek water on Colleen's face.

Colleen frowned at him. She wished Pa could take Jeb with him. He was out cutting wild hay for fodder. But no, Jeb was too little. Colleen put down the shirt and walked over to him. She snatched the stick, threw it away and grabbed for his arm. He ran out into the water and crossed the creek.

"You better run," she yelled. Jeb darted behind willows at the bend in the creek and disappeared.

Colleen sighed and looked at the sky. A wedge of geese moved slowly in the distance traveling south. "Geese, Ma!" Colleen called. Ma smiled back at her, and Colleen watched the geese. And then Ma talked about a new winter dress for Colleen. Burgundy-colored. When Colleen bent over Bonnie's basket and told her about the geese and the dress, Bonnie stopped sucking on her hand and listened. Colleen breathed in the clean, cool air, felt the warm sun on her face. It would have been a fine day if Jeb was not still mad.

The work went slowly. Cinder was barking across the creek. Colleen and Ma glanced that way. Jeb was there, too, running about, and Colleen noticed something sparkling in his hand, catching a glint of sun.

The watch?

Not the watch! He wouldn't have gotten the watch out. Colleen stood up and started toward the creek.

"Where do you think you're going?"

Colleen looked back at Ma. What could she say? Jeb was almost out of sight again behind some trees. So Colleen went back to her rinsing.

If Jeb had the watch, she'd get it back after the laundry was done. She rinsed clothes and lay them out on bushes, and she kept an eye out for her little brother.

Later he came splashing though the creek. There was no sign of the watch. He told Ma about some animal tracks he'd seen, and he glared at Colleen. She turned her head back to her work. She tried to think about the new dress, but Jeb's anger nagged at her.

As soon as she saw the place she had buried the watch, she knew Jeb had been there. Or someone had. The ground was soft, recently moved, and the old crockery jar was almost sticking out from under a thin layer of dirt. The watch was gone.

JEB WAS UP IN THE HAYLOFT, and Cinder was on the barn floor below him. A rope dangled from Jeb's dusty little hands.

Colleen grabbed the rope and yanked it down. She glared up at him.

"The watch! You took it!" she said. She hushed her voice, glanced to the opening and back up at Jeb. "Where is it?"

Jeb shook his head again and again. "I don't have it."

Colleen grabbed the thick rough rungs leading to the loft and climbed up.

"Then tell me what you had at the creek. You had something shiny in your hand. Tell me that, Jeb . . . ," Colleen began.

Jeb would not answer. He stared defiantly at her.

Colleen took a deep breath. "Don't you see?" she whispered loudly. "The watch is a secret. If someone finds it, we'll have to give it back. You want Bonnie to have it, don't you?"

Jeb studied her. He was quiet for a minute. Colleen picked at her fingernails. He understands, she thought.

He did not understand.

"No!" he yelled at her. "I don't have it."

"You do! I know you do!" Colleen shouted back. Jeb was a blur to her. She wiped her eyes clear of the angry tears. "I showed you the watch. And now you're so stupid you're going to ruin it. You *tell* me where you put it right now."

"No! . . . And I won't ever tell you. And you'll never find it either."

She crawled across the hay-covered planks, but Jeb scurried away into a little dark corner under the rafters. Colleen followed on her knees. She tried to search his shirt pocket.

She stared at him, bewildered.

Jeb jumped up. He scurried down the rungs and jumped to the floor of the barn.

"I'm gonna tell Ma and Pa about you and all your old secrets!" He glared up at Colleen and disappeared out the barn door. "And they won't like it, either!" he yelled.

"Colleen!" It was Ma. Colleen turned in that direction. It must be the pickles. Ma had told her she was going to need her help soon making pickles.

Colleen climbed down and jumped to the ground. Outside she looked for Jeb. He was running out toward the south ridge. Colleen squinted. Pa was out that way. Far out there with the scythe.

Ma's voice again. Colleen ran to the cabin. Ma took

one look at Colleen's flushed face, Colleen's dark eyes flashing angrily back out the door.

"Don't you bring that face in here," Ma said. "And how did you get that hay in your hair?"

"Jeb . . . ," Colleen answered. She bit her tongue. *He's going to grow up to be a heathen,* she dared not add.

At the front door Colleen bent over and dusted her hair outside. And inside again, she kept her mouth shut. The baby began to cry. Colleen went and picked her up and kissed her sweet little face. She looked at Jeb's little bed behind the stove.

He was just a little boy. And he was not bad. This was her fault. She was the one growing up to be a heathen.

She would have to get Jeb to give the watch back. She would have to make him understand he could not take chances with the watch.

She would have to tell Jeb the truth.

OCTOBER WAS COMING. Indian grass had long since started turning gold. Gulls were in the skies and the first of the Canada geese. Bright sunlight warmed the day, but when Colleen breathed in, she could smell the chill of fall in the air. It was the morning Colleen told Jeb the truth.

She found him playing at the creek.

"Jeb!" Colleen called, running down the little twisting path.

Jeb stood out on a flat rock in the middle of the creek. He looked her way. Colleen stopped at the water's edge.

"I'm not going to fuss . . . ," she said. She watched him, and then waded out to the rock. "Jeb?" she said. She reached out and touched his arm.

"I have a secret to tell you." She stooped down to sit on the giant rock. "Sit down here and I'll tell."

Jeb gave her a quick look and looked back at the water.

"Remember I told you I'd tell you more about the watch when you were bigger? Well, I decided not to wait. . . . It's time you know now."

Colleen squinted up in the bright sun at her little brother. Behind him dazzling yellow cottonwoods stood against the wind. Jeb sat down. Colleen gave him a long look. "You must never tell anyone, Jeb. Never." They sat there and Colleen told Jeb about everything she did the night Ma had the baby, and how it came about that they now had little Bonnie.

"She's ours?" Jeb said. "The wagon woman baby's ours?" Jeb said.

"Now she is. Her mother gave her to us. But it's a secret . . ."

"And Ma's baby died?"

"Ma's baby, she was too little . . ."

They were quiet for a while, quiet in the sun, and it warmed them. They jumped off the rock and waded in the middle of the creek, and cold water moved slowly around their ankles, flowing downstream toward the big, muddy river.

"Why can't we tell Ma and Pa, Colleen?"

Colleen bent over and looked into his eyes. "Jeb . . ." She swallowed hard. "Ma and Pa'd go by the law. They're grown up. They would think that was the only thing they could do. They would, Jeb. And the law'd tell them they had to give Bonnie back."

Jeb looked intently at Colleen. He looked confused.

"If we tell them, it'd be like making them tell the law.

They don't want to do that. It'd break their hearts. . . . See?"

Jeb thought about it. He nodded, and Colleen stood up.

"You tell me where the watch is. So I can hide it good," she said.

"I can't tell you. It's in my secret hiding place," Jeb said.

Colleen squinted at Jeb. He could have hidden it someplace Ma or Pa would find it.

"You don't have to show me your hiding place. You just get the watch for me. And we can hide it together. All right?"

"I'll get it," Jeb said. "But don't you look where I go. You close your eyes and count to a hundred."

He was going to give it back! Colleen put her hands over her eyes and started counting. "And you bring it right back here, Jeb!" she called before counting on as fast as she could and she got to one hundred. She opened her eyes.

"Jeb!" Colleen called. She looked around. "Jeb?!" Colleen called again, and then she stopped. He couldn't hear her anymore.

She glanced over her shoulder. At the top of the bank, some tall grasses swayed, and a deep blue September sky glowed. She looked upstream and down. Tomorrow she'd ask Ma if she could take Jeb with her to the post office. And by the blacksmith's. He'd like that. Maybe take him down to the river. If Ma said that was all right.

And then Colleen stopped and looked down the creek.

"No . . . ," she whispered.

She began to run downstream. The rock. The rock where they'd seen the rattlers.

It was all right, though. Colleen stopped to catch her breath. She'd told him that wasn't a good place. She'd convinced him. She was sure she had.

She ran downstream again, and she stopped and turned to look back up the creek where she'd come from. Jeb was not there. "Jeb!" He wasn't anywhere. She ran again, and she told herself that just because they'd seen a couple of rattlers at that rock before, rattlers wouldn't be there now. Surely not. My goodness, it wasn't like you could just go to that place, go to that big rock and sure enough there'd be a rattler every time.

She ran on. She was being silly, she told herself over and over. Everything was all right. It was almost October. The snakes would be moving toward their dens in October. Her feet splashed through the chilled water, and she tripped and fell and then she was up again running.

Almost there. Almost there. Colleen stopped dead in her tracks. She stood in the edge of the creek. Jeb was sitting in the water squeezing his left wrist with his other hand. He looked at her, crying.

And she saw the rattler.

It slid along the bank, the sun shining on its blotched back, and disappeared.

COLLEEN RAN TO HER brother and grabbed his hand. There wasn't much blood. But she saw two fang marks.

Jeb *had* hidden the watch here. It lay on the ground beside him. Colleen took it and pushed it in the pocket on her pinafore.

"It hurts." Jeb sniffled.

Colleen tried to remember. What had Pa said? She took her apron off and tied one of the strings around Jeb's arm. Not too tight. She found her knife.

"Are you going to cut it!" Jeb asked. He choked on a sob.

"I've got to get the poison out!"

"I want Ma."

Should she go? Try to get Ma? It was too far, wasn't it? She was supposed to get the poison out, wasn't she?

Colleen placed the blade on the fang marks.

"No!" Jeb squealed. "I don't want you to do it. Get Ma to! She'll know how!" Jeb's face was red.

"Jeb . . . Ma's too far off. I know what to do."

She stared again at the bite marks. She had to do this.

She would do this. And every part of her ached under her skin when she cut.

"Ooowww!"

"You want me to get the poison out, Jeb . . ."

She sucked out the poison and spit. Over and over. She did not care if the poison made her sick.

Jeb's hand was swelling and turning blue.

"I want Ma!"

Maybe someone was around. "Help!" Colleen screamed.

Silence.

"Is somebody here? Help! Somebody!"

"I want Ma! Go get Ma!"

What to do? Was the poison out? Should she go get somebody?

Colleen tried to get more venom out of the cut.

"I don't feel good. I want Ma," Jeb cried.

Should she go? Should she?

Colleen's chest felt tight. She didn't know how long it had been. Maybe she'd better get help. Maybe the poison was out.

"I'm going to go get somebody," Colleen told Jeb. "You wait here . . . and don't move."

Jeb curled over on his side holding his wrist with his other hand, his face scrunched up. "It hurts," he whimpered.

"Remember what Pa said. Don't move . . ." Colleen

stood up. Her mouth felt funny. She didn't care. "Don't move. Understand? Jeb?" She looked at him a moment more.

Colleen climbed as fast as she could to the top of the ravine. A stand of Indian grass waved golden and straight ahead of her. The Stockdale cabin beyond it, half a mile away. She could see it, could see Mr. O'Brien at the corral, too. She ran until she could not breathe and waved her hands over her head.

CLAY O'BRIEN HITCHED the Appaloosa up to an
old buckboard and put Jeb in the back with
Colleen. The wagon moved across the prairie, creaking,
jostling, and Colleen held Jeb's head in her lap. The blue
skin turned darker around the bite, and Jeb's hand, and
his arm, too, were swelling more.

"Don't worry too much about them prairie rattlers,"
Mr. O'Brien shouted back at Jeb. "Why, these little bug-
gers aren't like the big rattlers back east."

Colleen was grateful to Mr. O'Brien for fetching Jeb
from the ravine and saying things to make Jeb feel better. And Colleen knew that what he said was true. But a
person could die still. And Jeb was so little. Jeb was holding on to Colleen's skirt with one stubby little hand. And
the other hand was swollen more than before.

"Cinder got bit by a snake last summer," Colleen
said. She tried to make her voice like Mr. O'Brien's. Sure.
But she was scared. Her heart was aching inside, she was
so scared.

Mr. O'Brien went for the doctor so Pa could be at

home with Jeb. But the doctor was in Yankton. A day's trip there. Another day back.

The doctor would not come in time. Jeb would have to make it on his own. Ma and Pa told Colleen she did the right thing.

They did not know.

Colleen sat on her bed and tried to be brave. She gripped the edge of her straw tick. She loosed her hands and put them in her lap. She was quiet. She loved her little brother.

Her little brother whose whole arm was swollen within hours. Whose pulse was fast and fluttery and weak.

The venom of the snake left Jeb complaining of numbness in his mouth and numbness on his lips and a taste like metal. And Colleen stood behind Ma, both hands twirling one strand of hair around and around. Watching. Praying to the Lord to let Jeb live. She helped Ma and Pa, doing what she was told.

For two days and two nights Colleen would not sleep.

Around twilight on the second day it got hard for Jeb to breathe. Colleen brought him water, but he was sick to his stomach when he tried to drink it.

Colleen backed away, leaving Ma and Pa to comfort him. She leaned into the shadows against the wall. Her pinafore hung on its peg there. She remembered the watch in the pocket.

The watch her little brother had gone after. For her. Colleen looked quickly back at Jeb. Ma's hand was on his face, checking him for fever. Colleen slipped the watch out into her hand and squeezed it. Cool. Heavy. She held it and it warmed in her hand. She went to sit on her bed, and she pushed the watch deep under her pillow. Later, she would return it to the hiding place in the ravine.

The night trailed on. Bonnie began to cry.

Colleen went to check on her. "Hey, baby," she said. And Bonnie stopped crying. She turned her head and her eyes followed Colleen moving above the cradle.

Colleen changed her and carried her back to the rocker where she sat holding her tight and humming to her, still watching, still praying.

She wondered when the doctor would come. And she wondered about the wagon man. About him helping. It was kind of him to bring Jeb home, to go for the doctor. Those things Colleen had welcomed. She supposed there were men of some sort who would leave a little boy hurt out on the prairie. But that was not what she imagined this man to be.

Yet she remembered Mary Kathleen O'Brien's fingers gripping her arm. *He can change in a heartbeat. Like a wounded animal.* Colleen believed that, too.

Little Bonnie went to sleep quickly, and Colleen kissed her and put her back in her cradle. Then she went again to stand behind her mother.

The snake was long gone, disappeared into the prairie ravines. It never knew what damage it had done. Colleen did not blame the snake. She knew whose fault this had been.

Jeb did live.

The second night the doctor got there. Mr. O'Brien had sent him on but remained in Yankton himself. And by that time the pain had lessened. By the next morning Jeb was over the worst of it.

That night the coyotes sang.

Songdogs.

It had been a wondrous day. Ma and Colleen had fussed over Jeb, spoiling him. He had sat in the rocker. Pale. His eyes bright. And after supper Colleen was too happy to sleep. When the candles were lit she went outside, and folded her arms across the fence, and listened to the night.

The moon had risen further in the sky so that it cast a whitish light over the prairie. The land lay still and quiet. Only the sound of the coyotes. Just their songs drifting in the wind under the faraway stars.

T HE SETTLEMENT HAD been busy. Colleen could see dust when she looked toward the river. Some men from the ranch east of there, she figured, their horses churning up dust. She turned Shine toward the post office.

The postmaster had a message for Colleen. The Widow Jones wanted her to drop by on her way home. He gave Colleen a letter for Ma from her sister Kate and one for the widow, too.

Colleen frowned. It was October now, and she had hoped to go down to the river. Maybe the mallards were there. Maybe the first of the snow geese. But now she had to go by the widow's. Now there wouldn't be time.

So Colleen rode away into the grasses, dry with autumn, grasses turned to gold and wine, and she wondered what the widow wanted. Maybe she had some little treat for Jeb, something to gladden his day, Colleen hoped.

She crossed a shallow ravine and neared the widow's place, the cabin and outbuildings, dim specks in the late sunlight, and she eased Shine to a stop a good distance off.

A lost wind swept by, lifting Shine's mane and making the grasses bow in its way. She watched. She should get on her way. But she waited.

The widow asked Colleen to come in. Colleen had rarely been inside the widow's cabin and she looked around eagerly. It was dark but there were two bright little windows. It was a little larger than most. A mahogany table and chairs, a marble-top cabinet, a piano, a large mirror.

The widow certainly had plenty, Colleen thought. Ma would say not to be envious. Well, she had enough wrongdoings to worry about without being envious. But she liked the widow's cabin. She liked the hewn walls, and plank floors, and she liked the fine things.

Pa and Ma might just build a cabin like this someday. After the herd was built up.

"Why don't you sit down?" the widow said.

Colleen sat in a pretty chair. "Oh . . . the postmaster . . . he sent this along for you," Colleen said, standing back up. She held out a letter. The widow put it in a wooden box. The box was like the other things, beautiful, with a carving of leaves and flowers on its top. There was money in the box.

Colleen sat back down. They looked at each other.

Colleen found herself folding Aunt Kate's letter back and forth, twisting at it and folding it in two. She straightened it out again and put her hands flat on top of it, and she took a deep breath and smiled at the widow.

"Do you like tea, Colleen? Would you like some tea?"

"Oh! Yes!" Colleen said. "I would." The widow went to the stove to get the tea.

Colleen got up herself and went to the piano. She looked back toward the stove before putting her fingers on the cool white keys. She guessed she shouldn't push one down. Not without asking. But if she pushed one softly . . . that would be fun. Colleen put a finger on one key and pushed it down. Very slowly. And another and this time it played a note. A pretty single note. Colleen swirled around. The widow was coming back with two cups. The widow smiled, and Colleen laughed and smiled back.

The widow wasn't bad.

"How's little Jeb?" Widow Jones asked. "Everyone was so worried."

"He's fine now," Colleen said. "He's his old self. Pa says now we know how tough he is . . . now a rattler can't kill him. Jeb likes that." Colleen laughed.

She took a sip of the tea. It tasted beautiful. "Thank you for the tea," Colleen said. "It's wonderful!"

The widow was glad. Colleen began to look around the room again, and she wondered should she go? Why had the widow asked her to come? Colleen stood up. "I better go," she said.

"Colleen?"

Colleen's heart felt cool inside. Something in the widow's tone had changed.

"Yes, ma'am?"

"I . . . don't know quite how to say this but . . . some things that have happened and . . . things you've said, trouble me . . . I can't seem to stop worrying over them."

Colleen wanted to go. Now.

"I told myself . . . just talk to the girl," Widow Jones hesitated, looked straight at Colleen. "Is that all right?"

No. It was not all right. Colleen put her teacup down on a table.

It wasn't fair bringing her here, then asking questions.

She glanced up at the widow and nodded.

"About the baby, Colleen. Your mother wasn't due. Yet Bonnie was not underweight. Well, you know everything I'm saying . . . and the things you told me that night and in the days after, you told the O'Brien man differently . . . A different story."

She knows, Colleen thought.

She looked at the door. She wanted to run, but she looked back toward the widow. The wind was making a buzzing sound in a window frame. She wished it would stop.

"I really don't know any other way to say this . . ." The widow took a breath. "Except to come right out with it." She peered at Colleen.

"Colleen, did you switch the babies that night? Was your mother's baby stillborn . . . and did you switch them?"

Colleen stared at the widow. She felt weak, drained. Her blood must be draining right out of her heart.

She is just guessing, Colleen thought. *She does not know this.*

And suddenly Colleen's eyes were shining with tears, and she shook her head. "No . . . that's not what happened," she whispered.

And for some time there was no sound except the continual wind buzzing in the windowpane. She took steps backward toward the door.

"Well . . . in that case," the widow said. "In that case . . . we will forget I spoke of this."

Colleen went to the door. She looked back. "It's not true," she said. "What you said. It isn't."

And then she ran from that house.

Colleen ran to Shine. She led him down the tiny road

past dried sunflower stalks long since butter-colored in the summer, and turned in through rows of dried brown Indian corn.

The rows became a path through the wild grass. Colleen climbed up on Shine and rode across the prairie toward the setting sun, toward the ravine, to get away.

When they were a half-mile off, Colleen stopped and looked back at the widow's house and the little panes looked like they were on fire, brightly lit by the late afternoon sun. She squinted at the tiny glow of a house, so still in the waving grass and brushed her windblown hair out of her face.

"She does not know," Colleen whispered to herself. "She will not speak of it again."

She did not head straight home, crossing the sweep of grasses in a northwesterly direction, but rode west, doglegging toward the next creek and then following the edge of the break.

In time Colleen came upon the wagon, strangely bright against the darkening of huge gray clouds in the east. Its canvas, torn loose by the wind, tossed there, reaching out to the prairie sky. Surely soon that part would rip off and sail into the sky, into the clouds. Across the trails of birds.

Colleen stopped the horse and watched the wagon in

the smoky blue quiet, and the winds whispered through the grass. A ribbon of wild geese drifted away in the sky, and she remembered the woman who had given her Bonnie.

Whispers and wind and a lace trim collar. Pale, sallow skin and green eyes and a prayer. *Thank you, Lord, for sending this prairie child here.* A little smile then. She had looked at Colleen then. Colleen had not forgotten. Colleen would never forget.

IN THE MORNING Colleen saw more geese. Long, trembling wedges of geese edging their way south. The horses and cattle grazed on the open prairie, and goldenrod speckled the land.

Colleen and Jeb went to the creek. Jeb wanted to see the watch again. He wanted to carry it around in his pocket for the day.

That was not such a big thing to ask. It would be mean to say no. Colleen had taken to saying yes to Jeb, to most everything since the bite. And she told him yes now.

The watch was there in the ravine. Back in the buried crock jar. Where it would be safe. Colleen got the watch out and put it in Jeb's hand. She smiled at him. It made her feel good. She left him there with the watch and hurried back to finish her chores.

After rocking Bonnie to sleep, Colleen went to chase a chicken out of the barn. She found the hen pecking behind the shovel in the corner and grabbed it. It flapped its wings but she held on, and when Colleen looked around, there was Jeb's dark little figure between her and the sunny barn door opening. Thousands of bits of shining hay dust sprinkled the air around him.

She almost left for the barnyard. But there was something about the way he stood there . . .

"What?" Colleen asked, still holding tightly to the hen. And then she saw.

Pa was there too, come to stand there in the barn door beside Jeb, and Colleen dropped the chicken to the earth. The chicken ran off squawking. Colleen looked up at Pa's face. Her eyes fell to the golden watch in Pa's hand. It dangled from its golden chain by his side shining in the sun, and Colleen looked again at her pa's face.

"How did you come by this watch?" Pa asked.

Colleen's eyes played between Pa and the watch dangling there in the shaft of sun and for a moment she could not speak.

"The wagon woman . . . ," she said. She looked helplessly at Pa. He waited. Colleen swallowed hard. "In the wagon, Mr. O'Brien's wife, I told her Ma had just had a baby. That I was looking for help. . . . She told me to take it for Bonnie. She wanted Bonnie to have it."

Pa looked again at the watch, gathered the chain up in his hands and opened the watch, closed it carefully. He handed it back to Jeb.

Colleen clutched her bottom lip between her teeth, breathing hard, still looking at the watch, and her eyes were shining with tears.

They stood there for a while, and Cinder bounded into the barn, and he nipped at Jeb's heels and still Pa said nothing. Cinder sat down, wagged his tail, thumping it there on the earth. In a while Pa turned his head away and looked out at the land.

"You go in and you tell your ma about this."

"I will, Pa," Colleen said.

"Pa?" Jeb asked, looking up at Pa.

"You too," Pa said to Jeb. He looked again at Colleen.

Is it all right, she wanted to say. . . . *Do you forgive me,* she wanted to say. . . . She picked at her thumbnail and watched her pa. His eyes. Shadowed. Puzzled. Unable to understand. And then he left. Colleen followed him to the barn door and stopped there and watched her pa walking back out to the fields.

The cabin sat quietly in the sun, and a tiny hint of smoke from the stovepipe disappeared in the wind. Cinder was dashing about toward a small dry wash past the corn, and the sky was a darkening blue there. It was the kind of deep-colored October sky Colleen loved.

Ma was in the cabin just putting Bonnie in her cradle. Colleen stopped in the doorway, Jeb behind her. Colleen scratched mindlessly on her elbow. She stopped and squeezed one hand in the other.

Colleen told Ma the same story she had just told Pa. And it was partly true, Colleen told herself. But she knew partly true made it a lie.

So now, finished with the story, Colleen looked at the floor, the puncheon floor Pa had put in that past winter, and the wind whistled at the eaves. A goose outside fluttered its wings. Colleen hung her head.

"You look at me, Colleen McCall," Ma said.

Colleen's eyes peeped up and met Ma's angry ones.

"Why did you lie to that man when he came over here?"

"The woman wanted Bonnie to have it," Colleen said softly.

Ma sat Colleen on the stool till Pa came back in at suppertime. And Jeb had to stay inside too.

Later, after supper, after the candles were lit and glimmering in the cabin, Colleen leaned against the wall and held the sleeping baby and watched her family, watched Ma at the stove, watched Pa cleaning the rifle at the table, watched Jeb rolling on the floor with Cinder. And remembered the voice. Pa's voice . . .

In his voice Colleen heard an anger she had never heard before. It frightened her. He didn't give her a whipping. He must have been too angry to give her a whipping.

Or maybe he thought twelve was getting too old for a whipping.

Colleen held the baby a little tighter. "I don't care. I don't care. I won't ever let anyone take you away," she whispered ever so quietly, and her eyes darted to Ma and Pa as if somehow they could hear her secret silent words. Outside the wind struck soft hollow tones in the bell-chimes, and Colleen closed her lips tightly.

Bonnie began to coo. Colleen sat in the rocker and laid the baby down in her lap. She bent over and looked in Bonnie's deep blue eyes. "You are a good, good little baby," Colleen said.

Across the grasslands the quiet wind rushed on. A whisper wind, Colleen thought. If only the wind could carry her secret away and hide it forever on a dim and silver star.

THE NEXT MORNING Pa told Colleen that as soon as breakfast was done, she would take the watch back to Mr. O'Brien. He would go with her.

Colleen was speechless. The watch was Bonnie's, but she dared not say anything.

They walked. A mile there. Colleen walked behind her pa through the tall grass near the edge of the break carrying Bonnie's golden watch. There was a haze in the ravine, and Colleen wanted to ask Pa if there weren't fires around somewhere. It was the time of year for them. Smoke from fires somewhere far out on the prairie would collect in ravines. But she dared not say anything.

Two men were there at the cabin with Mr. O'Brien. Colleen squinted. Probably some river men. It looked like they had plowed a firebreak and were getting ready to burn it. Three furrows circling the buildings. The haze in the ravine. She'd been right. There was fire around.

Pa and Mr. O'Brien stepped off a ways in the grass. Colleen stood back and watched. Mr. O'Brien took off his hat, pushed his hand through his hair. Pa said something. He motioned to Colleen, and she ran to him.

Colleen handed Mr. O'Brien the watch. "I'm sorry. I'm sorry I didn't tell you about this . . . when you came," she stammered, looking up at Mr. O'Brien. "Your wife gave it to me . . . for our baby."

The man said nothing. He turned the shining gold thing about in his hand, examining it, and Colleen looked at her pa.

"I don't abide by this," Pa said. Clay O'Brien looked at Pa and at Colleen.

"There was more . . . ," Clay O'Brien said. "More things missing."

"Is there anything else, Colleen?" Pa said then, surprising her. "Anything else that you took from there?"

He had not asked her that at home. It must not have occurred to him till now. Even with the watch, it must have not occurred to him.

She glanced up at her pa.

She wished he had not asked her. She stood there silent.

"Colleen?"

Colleen hung her head. "Nothing," she said, and she felt her face burning.

"She's done this sort of thing before?" Mr. O'Brien asked.

Pa shook his head. "Never.

"If there's nothing else . . . ," Pa said.

Clay O'Brien looked at Colleen, scowling, then raised one hand in dismissal.

"Bid you 'day then," said Pa. The man nodded, and Pa strode away then, and Colleen could see Pa's shame over her.

A sudden breeze tumbled Colleen's hair. She watched her pa leaving and she started to run after him. But something stopped her. And she looked back unsure, looked back up at Clay O'Brien.

She started to say something. Maybe she could make him understand the watch *was* a gift.

He smiled. Then the smile dissolved.

"My wife was dead when you got there, wasn't she?" he said. "And you never counted on me showing up. That innocent face . . . Nobody'd dream you'd rob the dead. Nobody but me."

Rob the dead, Colleen thought. Mary Kathleen had said those words. *Rob the dead.* Words Colleen had tried to remember. *Is that what you did, Mr. O'Brien? It is, isn't it?* Robbed the dead in the war for that money.

Colleen backed away from him, confused. The other two men were coming that way. "I didn't take the watch, Mr. O'Brien. Your wife was alive, and she gave it to me," she said, squinting back at him in the bright sun.

She turned and ran toward where Pa was waiting in the golden grass, but she could still hear the men behind her. And before she got to Pa, she heard Clay O'Brien call someone a little fool.

T HEY SAW THE GLOW from the prairie fire that
night, reflected on the northwest edge of the black
sky. And for two more nights they saw it, each night
brighter than the last. Closer.

Pa said lightning most likely started it, the dry autumn grasslands, tinder now. Just waiting.

Last year fire had come earlier. From the west. Black
smoke on the horizon, blocking out the sun. It had come
fast. Jumping one creek bed, so strong was the wind that
day. But not their creek. The wind had died off. Pa and
the other men had started a backfire on the other side of
the ravine. Colleen had watched that backfire. It had
moved away toward the great fire out on the prairie,
burning all the grass in its way and then the prairie fire
could not burn there. They had beat out all traces of
flames on their side. She had helped. That fire had
missed them.

Now the family stood on the ridge north of the corn-
field and watched. The night air was cool, and the dry-
ing corn rustled quietly behind them.

"Might be fifteen, twenty miles off," Pa said. "Maybe more."

Colleen tried squinting her eyes, but there were no flames to see. The flames were below the horizon.

Jeb tugged on Pa's sleeve. "Will it come here?"

"Maybe not."

Colleen wondered. The ravines could not stop this fire if it came at them from the north, between the breaks. But Pa thought they'd be safe. They had time.

Well, Colleen thought, she was glad fire had come. She thought that, but she caught herself. No. Of course not. The fire was exciting. As long as it was over there. Especially at night. But she was not glad.

Ma said it was good that Pa and Mr. Newman and Mr. Russert had burned the firebreaks around the cabins back in July. "But," Ma said, "I don't like it hovering over there. It gives me a nervous feeling."

"It shouldn't be bad . . . as long as we don't get any wind, we'll be all right," Pa said.

Pa and Ma talked more. Pa would be plowing more firebreaks around the stackyards. "Newman and Russert too," he said. They would be helping each other burn them.

Colleen kept looking north. The Russert and Newman farms were out there. The fire would go past them first. And then here. And then the Stockdale place. Passing by each of the little farms lining the creek on its way down to the big river. Pa said he thought it'd die down and go out before it ever got to the river.

Pa went to check on the horses then, and Bonnie was beginning to cry. "Oh, my," Ma said. "Let me get back to my little Bonnie." And Ma went back inside and left the children by themselves.

They watched, mesmerized, and for a while neither spoke a word.

"If it does come here, will it burn up our cabin?" Jeb asked.

"No."

"Why not?"

" 'Cause there's not any wind."

"Are there people way out there?"

Colleen did not answer. She stared at the red-orange light far across the boundless prairie. She *was* glad this fire was out there. She was.

"Are there? Are there people out there?"

"I don't think so."

She tightened her brows. She was not glad if anybody got hurt. She was not glad if any animals got hurt. But every fall the fires came. And part of her was glad this one was here now. And she knew she was wicked for thinking that. But the truth was, the fire put Pa's and Ma's minds on something other than her lies.

Beyond the edge of the prairie in the dark quiet the fire burned on, too far for their eyes to see. The swishing of the corn leaves all but stopped. Ma's bell-chimes sounded once, a hushed tone, but to Colleen, they seemed bells out of tune.

A FEW DAYS AFTER COLLEEN took the watch back, Clay O'Brien came to the cabin. Colleen was inside watching Bonnie when she saw the man, O'Brien, standing in the doorway. The sun behind him, lighting only a thin shining edge of his figure.

"Where's your pa? Your ma?"

Colleen was taken off guard. "Out past the stack-yards," she said. "Pa's plowing furrows out there. . . . Ma's out there too. Out past the rise . . ."

He moved to leave.

"Why do you want them?" Colleen blurted out.

He looked back and considered her a moment. "You know why. Your pa's a fair man. Or I can get the law in here. Or maybe that widow woman knows more'n she's saying. One way or the other . . ."

"Ah!" Bonnie said. "Ah?" Colleen glanced toward her cradle and back to Mr. O'Brien. He just wanted the money. Just the money. He didn't know about the baby.

But the widow did.

He left the cabin then and headed toward the stack-yards.

The clock was ticking in the quiet over on the sideboard. A quarter of a minute passed. Colleen scooped Bonnie up and ran after him. "The widow doesn't know anything," she yelled.

The man kept walking, paying her no mind.

The widow might talk. Might tell about the baby. If Ma and Pa asked her. If the law asked her.

"Don't tell them!" Colleen cried.

She stopped.

"I'll get it. I'll get the box. I'll give it back," she said quietly.

Clay O'Brien turned and looked at her.

Colleen held the baby tighter. "I will," she said.

Mr. O'Brien waited in the sunny barnyard.

"I don't have it here. But I'll bring it to you. By the end of the week."

She stood, shifting from foot to foot with the baby chewing on her little hand, her blue eyes wide, and Colleen watched Clay O'Brien.

"Tomorrow . . . ," he said finally.

Clay O'Brien left them then. Bonnie and Colleen. Colleen looked over toward the stackyards. She could not see Ma or Pa or Jeb.

She watched Clay O'Brien riding away, hints of the black horse wavering in the yellow grass. More geese were in the sky, far far above them, up on some high angel wind. Colleen watched the geese.

"Ah? Ah!" said Bonnie. And she waved her arms, and Colleen kissed the top of her head and stared out at the grass. Too many miles of grass. Her eyes swept the edges of the prairie. She had looked and looked out there. *She could not find the box.*

On the ridge Ma's figure passed between the tops of two haystacks. Disappeared again. And Colleen's heart beat harder, beat quicker.

There was forty-seven dollars inside the cabin. Money for salt, or ammunition, or a new harness. Her brows tightened.

Or for Bonnie?

Her eyes flickered toward the cabin. She took a quick deep breath, and glanced toward the stackyards. The sun gleamed off the tops of the haystacks, off the top of Jeb's hair as he darted between them. Colleen started back to the cabin still looking that way.

Inside, she put Bonnie in her cradle.

She could take the money.

But that would be wrong. She walked to the door. And stood there with her fingers to her mouth.

No matter what, she had told Mary Kathleen O'Brien . . . she had promised.

Colleen looked back toward the wardrobe where the money stayed. Again, a sickening rush of blood, inside her, under her skin.

She ran to the wardrobe and knelt there and lifted the planks, and under them she saw the money. She looked over her shoulder. She felt sick.

Exodus. Chapter 20. Thou shalt not steal. She had learned the verse when she was little. Back in Pennsylvania. No good can come from going against the Lord's commandments, Ma always said.

But Colleen did not want to listen to those thoughts. She pushed the thoughts away.

Colleen wanted to *do* something.

So Colleen took the money. Squeezed it in her hand. Pushed the planks back down in place and ran to the door.

Maybe she wouldn't give this to Clay O'Brien, she told herself. And she could look again for the box this afternoon. She might find it. She might, she told herself.

At supper, Pa talked about the fire.

Mr. Russert had ridden out that way. No wind to speak of yet. Mr. Russert said fires up that way could burn for weeks before anybody'd even see flames down where their farms were.

Colleen did not care about the fire. It was just like last year. Not even as bad. The fire would not take Bonnie away.

"It's moving in this direction now, but slow," Pa said. "It'll burn winter range."

But Colleen did not want to think about winter range. Pa had lots of hay. The horses. The cattle. They would be all right. Colleen thought about Mr. O'Brien and Bonnie and about the money. . . . Forty-seven dollars that was now stuffed in her pinafore pocket. But what if there had been a hundred dollars in that box? Wasn't that what the man had said when he first came to their cabin? Then forty-seven dollars would not be enough.

SOMETIME BEFORE DAWN Pa and Ma were up. The fire was closer. But still there was no wind. Colleen and Jeb ran outside in their nightclothes, smelling smoke, looking for fire. Only trails of white smoke. Haze dimming the early sky. They did not see fire.

Paul Russert came by. He and Pa talked. Colleen was sent over to the widow's to ask if she knew anyone needing a hand down that way. Pa and the other men expected to finish in an hour or so. And could help then if need be. Colleen headed southeast on Shine. Straight across the smoky prairie toward the widow's.

And that was when the idea came to her. Not at first, not when she talked to the widow but later. Later when the widow had gone back out with her sons, gone far out past the barn.

Colleen rode Shine out into the yellow, rusty grasses on the other side of the widow's cabin. Firebreaks had been freshly plowed there and the grass between them already burned. Maybe yesterday. It was barely smoking. But Shine was ill at ease with the traces of smoke, and she stopped.

Shine flicked his ears, and Colleen patted his neck. The thought came to her then . . .

Suddenly.

The widow had money.

And she needed more money. Colleen looked back at the widow's cabin, pale in the haze.

No. What she took from home . . . that was bad enough. But stealing from a neighbor? What would that preacher say? And that hanging judge? This was law-breaking.

The wagon man was right. She might look innocent . . .

Still.

For Bonnie.

And she would pay it back. She would. Pa'd let her have some cows. She could carry extra milk to the settlement. She could do laundry for people. It would not make it right, she knew that, but she would work and make the money back.

There was not any time left. She had promised Clay O'Brien she'd give him the box today.

She left Shine there and she ran toward the back of the cabin and looked around the side. A trace of a breeze moved a stand of orange-red grass grown up wild by the barn.

She crept in the little back door. The room was quiet

and still, and Colleen saw the beautiful wooden box on a marble-top table. The beautiful carved box she had seen the money in.

She hesitated, her fingers up to her mouth. Maybe the widow would think she had misplaced it. Colleen dashed across the room. The money was there. Colleen took the money and stuffed it in her apron. Through the wobbly glass window she saw the widow walking between some haystacks.

Colleen backed away from the window.

There were tears on her cheeks. She did not want to do this. She did not want to be so hateful. But the widow would be all right. Her sons would see to that. She hesitated. She should put it back.

Out the window, far over on the ridge top, the widow stood in the haze. She turned, looked toward the house. Colleen stepped back farther.

"I promised Mary Kathleen," she whispered. "She was dying and I promised her and she believed me."

Out the window the small figures, the widow, her sons, moved slowly about. Colleen ran to the little door and carefully closed it behind her and raced back toward the wild dry grasses where she had left Shine.

Pa and Ma . . . if they knew . . . if they knew what all she'd done . . . She stopped running and looked back. She should go back . . . put the money back . . .

But no. No. She believed Mary Kathleen O'Brien.

So she kept on toward the horse.

She thought her heart might burst but she kept on running till she got to Shine and then she stopped and held on to the horse for a minute out of breath.

Everything back at the widow's looked still. No one was coming after her, no one had seen her. But inside her throat was a hard ache. The widow had done her no harm.

And still she got on the horse and rode away.

The O'Brien man will go away if he has the money, she told herself.

When Colleen got to the trail near the break, when she was out of sight of the widow's cabin, when she was hidden by shrubs, she stopped Shine and took the money out of her pocket. Ninety-three dollars from the widow. Forty-seven from home. Stolen. Every cent of it.

So that when she dreamed, she would not have to see the O'Brien man riding off with Bonnie into the hinterlands.

THE OLD STOCKDALE PLACE, its sagging cabin and outbuildings, lay low, partly hidden in the yellow grasses and haze. Before Colleen got there she heard voices. Clay O'Brien must be there. She and Jeb had seen him that morning, heading north on the black mare. But he must be back now.

A cloud of birds slid by, flew low, and Shine jumped and turned in a half circle. "Whoa . . . it's just birds. Easy, boy," Colleen said softly.

She listened. Everything was still. Quiet. Not even the whisper of the wind. But the air was heavy with smoke. Shine did not want to go. Finally Colleen jumped down and led the horse through the dry switchgrass and bluestem toward Clay O'Brien's, and she heard the voices again and stopped a moment. One sounded like a child's voice.

Like Jeb's voice.

When she got to where she could see the cabin, she saw that it *was* Jeb, Jeb and Cinder, standing over near an old plowshare that lay on the ground beside the barn door. Clay O'Brien was there too.

"Jeb, you should be home," Colleen said. "Does Ma know you're gone? She's not going to like this."

"I didn't want the spotted horse to burn up in the barn," Jeb told Colleen when he saw her. "I wanted to let it loose."

"Horse's all right, boy," Clay O'Brien said.

Jeb wrinkled his brows and stared at Clay O'Brien.

"It is, Jeb," Colleen whispered to him. She tilted her head quickly toward Shine. "Go wait for me."

Jeb did not go.

Colleen gave him a warning look. A light wind rippled through seed heads behind her. A whisper wind, but it bothered Colleen. It was coming from the north. She fumbled in her pinafore, pulling the money out. Jeb stared at it and up at her, amazed.

"Here," she said. She handed Mr. O'Brien the two rolled-up wads of bills.

Now. It would all end now. Surely the money was enough. Mr. O'Brien would go away now. She glanced at Jeb and back at the man. A hayfork leaned shiny and bright behind him against the old wall. He looked at the bills, unfolded them, counted them.

"And where is the rest?"

The rest?

Bewildered, Colleen stared at him. It wasn't enough? She was giving away part of her soul, stealing that money. And it wasn't enough?

"There was three hundred fifty dollars in that box . . . Where is it?"

Colleen stood staring at the money in the man's hands.

What could she say? The truth? He would not believe the truth. *He* knew. She did not tell the truth.

But he did not ask her again.

"Go on home . . . ," he said. His words were slow and quiet.

Colleen backed away but when she reached for Shine's reins, he twirled and scampered off a little distance, stopping to look back her way, tossing his head up and down.

Colleen glanced back at Clay O'Brien and again to the horse. "What's wrong?" she said to Shine. "You scared of smoke? It's just smoke . . . Come on . . ."

"I said get on home," Mr. O'Brien said. His hat brim hung low over his face. Loam clung to his pants and boots from the knees down. He flung his hand out in the direction of home as if to dismiss them.

"Go on. Now!" And his voice was loud then.

"Stop yelling at her!" Jeb said. "She gave you all that money. Now you leave our baby alone!"

No. Jeb . . . no . . . he doesn't know . . .

A horse nickered some ways off. One of Clay O'Brien's.

Colleen grabbed Jeb's hand and pulled him with

her toward Shine. Maybe Mr. O'Brien did not understand.

More birds swept by, low to the ground, and then rose again, and Shine bolted this time toward Clay O'Brien, and Clay O'Brien grabbed him by the halter.

"Baby?" Clay O'Brien said. "What you sayin', boy?"

"Hush, Jeb," Colleen said. She moved to get Shine.

"I say, what you talking 'bout, boy?"

"It's our baby! Bonnie! Her ma said so! She gave her to Colleen! She's ours . . . not yours." Jeb looked back at Colleen. "Tell him, Colleen . . ."

"Jeb . . . ," Colleen whispered.

The faint sound of a bell was clanging, somewhere far away, and Clay O'Brien was looking straight at Colleen.

"As I live I learn," he said. "So Kathleen was at it till the end." He chuckled and held out the reins toward Colleen, letting them fall loose.

Colleen snatched them, jumping in the saddle. She yelled at Jeb to come. She pulled him up and turned Shine and started toward the break.

"Tell your ma I'll be round for that young'un," Clay O'Brien called after them.

Colleen looked back, and she saw the man watching them and she saw him step back and vanish into the dark hole of the barn door. Mary Kathleen's wagon waited in the grass, fragile, balanced near the break, and a flock of small birds windled there in the sky.

Colleen turned Shine for home, and she felt a chilling thing in her heart.

FROM THE RIDGE PAST the Stockdale place, out to
the north, the prairie fire burned closer. The wind
was light, but the sky heavy with smoke. And the smoke
was darker now. It dried their throats. More birds moved
above them to the south. Still Colleen and Jeb had yet to
see flames.

At home the cattle were gathered near the barn, and
tiny mice, confused by the fire, darted through the grass.
Jackrabbits, too. Birds skimmed above the grass and
were gone.

For an instant Colleen sat there on the horse, and saw
her ma turn to look her way. Colleen held her breath.

She should *never* have waited till now.

"Ma!" she shouted. "I have to tell you something!"
She jumped from the horse then, and ran toward her
mother.

"Jeb McCall! Where on earth have you been?" Ma
scolded. "I told you to do your chores."

Jeb pointed back toward the O'Brien place and slid
off the horse.

"Ma!" Colleen said. She reached out for Ma's arm.

Ma shook her head, exasperated at Jeb, and turned to Colleen. "Your pa's back," she said. "I'm going to help him now. You watch Bonnie and keep an eye on the cabin and the barn. I don't think there'll be loose sparks, but you watch. Y'hear, Colleen? Ring the cowbell if you see any you can't put out. And there's something for you and Jeb to eat on the sideboard."

"But, Ma!" Colleen cried.

"You . . . " Ma looked back at Jeb. "Wet down your other pair of pants and bring them out to me. Then you come back and help your sister."

Ma looked at them then, her face drawn and tired. And she left the children there, and walked away on out past the corn to the edge of the open prairie. She would be beating out any sparks that jumped the firebreaks with wet cloth. Colleen watched her leaving, watched her ma's hair coming loose from its bun, trailing out, and Colleen did not run after her.

On the far horizon she saw the flames, a thin line of fire. Pa was out that way, closer. He'd be starting a backfire.

And Colleen knew she could scream the words out and make Ma listen. *Bonnie's not ours, Ma!* she could say. *She belongs to Mr. O'Brien, Ma! He's coming for her,* she could say.

But how could she say those words?

It seemed the wrong time.

Smoke darkened on the horizon, and a halting wind turned up loose straggles of Colleen's hair. Colleen frowned. When would Mr. O'Brien come? Now?

Bonnie was crying. Colleen ran inside to her cradle and wrapped her in her blanket. "We've got to go, Bonnie."

Pa had the horses in the corral, and Colleen found Jeb had gone in the barn with Shine. "I'm taking the baby to a safe place, safe from Mr. O'Brien," she told him.

"Where?" Jeb asked, and he followed Colleen outside.

"Over past the creek. This fire won't cross over there."

Colleen glanced to the open prairie.

A coyote moved into sight, out on the ridge, hunting ahead of the fire. Colleen watched and it disappeared suddenly in the taller grass, and she began to walk toward the ravine.

AT THE TOP OF THE ravine, Colleen stopped.
There were more birds, several of them sheering
near to the ground. Another jackrabbit. Other little grass
creatures. Smoke was thick down in the ravine.

Colleen looked northwest. A light wind whiffled
across the grasses. The fire would come only as fast as
the wind. Not fast.

Not if the wind stayed light.

It would burn slowly and might even miss the
Russerts' and the Newmans', both on twists of the creek
to the west before coming near home. Maybe the wind
would shift and miss home too, winding up dying out
over near the next break before it got to the widow's and
her people.

Colleen would not think about it anymore.

She would cross the creek. Climb up to the top of the
ravine on the other side. A place with thick shrubs. Up
on high ground. She could even start walking then, south
toward the river on the other side of the break. If the fire
came, it would not cross the break.

Colleen hurried down the little foot trail to the creek, waded through the cold water and followed the creek about a quarter of a mile thinking to get further away from the thickening smoke upstream. But she heard hoof-beats in water, against rock, and she stopped a moment and looked behind her up the creek. There was a willow thicket she could run to.

Colleen hurried there, holding Bonnie tightly. She crept between the thin willow trunks and stooped down where she could watch. To both sides she saw nothing moving save the tiny trickle of leaves passing in the slow creek water and stirrings made by the wind.

The wind, stronger but still uncertain, shifted the leaves in the willows momentarily, moved the tops of the cottonwoods, then quiet.

The horse and rider were there now.

Clay O'Brien. Colleen bit her lips and watched through the willows. She tried not to move. The horse was walking by the creek. O'Brien pulled the mare to a stop, and the horse began to drink. Was O'Brien heading to her cabin? Colleen wondered. It seemed an odd time, with the fire coming.

Bonnie made a tiny gurgle in her mouth and Colleen glanced at her then. "Shhh . . . ," she breathed, her eyes back on the man. He didn't seem to have heard.

But then, then Bonnie made a little cry. Colleen saw Clay O'Brien turn his head her way.

He swung off his horse. Colleen looked up the embankment behind her and back to him. He was walking toward her and the baby.

It was too late.

He stopped. He saw her. He saw her there in the thicket.

"Here I was maybe expecting some trouble out of your parents. After listening to your lying mouth, gal," he said. "But you're making it real easy."

"No!" Colleen shouted, standing up, holding Bonnie. "You can't take her!"

"Can't? Since when can't a man take his own flesh and blood?"

Colleen backed away clutching Bonnie, her right hand on Bonnie's head. But the ground behind the thicket was too steep. She stopped.

Clay O'Brien walked over to them. He put his hands around Bonnie, under Bonnie's little arms. Colleen watched Bonnie's little fingers curling. She saw Bonnie's little face wide-eyed. Confused. The man pulled the baby away and Colleen could have hung on tighter, but then he might have wrenched Bonnie away, and she did not want Bonnie to get hurt. She did not want Bonnie to be afraid so she did not hold on tighter. And now Clay O'Brien had Bonnie. And little Bonnie's face was startled, all crumpled up ready to cry.

"Let me keep her for you . . . till later . . ."

"Don't you worry, that Nelson woman down at the stage stop'll mind this young'un for me."

O'Brien turned and walked toward his horse. The baby he propped against his shoulder with one arm. Colleen stood breathless and watched. He wasn't listening to her.

"No!" Colleen ran after him. "Mary Kathleen! Mary Kathleen said for *me* to take the baby."

She grabbed at his arm crying, tried to shake him, tried to take Bonnie back. But with his free hand, O'Brien easily pried her hands loose. He shook his head. "You little fool." He looked hard at her. "All I want is the money. . . . You know where it is. The rest . . . the rest, I got no need of."

Bonnie?

Got no need of Bonnie? Colleen stepped back staring at the baby. And Bonnie, still in O'Brien's clutch, tried to turn her little face toward Colleen. Her little eyebrows raised. Puzzled.

O'Brien stood beside the great black mare. "You hear me?" he said.

Colleen nodded. She wiped the tears off her cheeks.

"Well, you listen then. Before sundown I'm following the wagon road . . . that one that comes up from Yankton. I'll be at Tackett Station tomorrow, after that Fort Randall. Tell your pa that . . . if he wants the young'un, he can find me. We'll make the switch. I don't want any trouble." O'Brien turned and started walking back downstream to the south, back toward the Stockdale place.

"Don't go! We can get the money . . ."

O'Brien walked away down the edge of the shallow creek. The trees were thinning of their leaves and minutes passed while Colleen stood frozen and watched before she ran, splashing across the creek and running after the wagon man and Bonnie until the smoke surrounded them and they disappeared around the curve of the creek. Then she stopped. She sank to her knees and sat back on her heels out of breath.

"Pa can sell the herd," she said quietly. "Would that be enough?"

There was a low grade down the creek that animals used. Not far. O'Brien would leave the ravine there. She could run. Maybe she could beat him there. If he was still walking the horse, she could. She would tell him Pa and Ma would sell the herd. She knew they would do that for Bonnie. And surely that would be enough. Maybe she could make him listen.

Her eyes were burning. She splashed them with creek water and got to her feet. She ran along the edge of the creek and stopped and stood and in the quiet, she heard O'Brien coughing. She heard the black horse nicker.

And in the quiet, she heard Bonnie begin to cry and her heart broke.

DOWNSTREAM WHERE Colleen had last seen Bonnie, she now saw smoke thick as fog. How could she have lost Bonnie? She should have held on tighter. She should have told Ma and Pa. Even if they hated her. She was just so afraid and she had promised. Tears started down her cheeks. Angrily she wiped them away. Tears would do no good now. The wagon man would not listen to her. She had to get Ma and Pa. This time she had to tell them.

Colleen scrambled to the top of the ravine and looked out across the prairie. But she could see nothing there past the broken ground and shrubs near the ravine. Smoke was thick and dark and burned her eyes.

The wind was up, coming from the north. The fire had surely passed the Newmans and the Russerts both by now. Her heart began to race.

But maybe it had not burned as far as home.

A jackrabbit bounded out of the shrubs, surprising her. She started walking, running toward home. Home. It was too smoky. She held her pinafore over her nose and mouth and coughed and coughed. In front of her she heard a deep, hollow, continuous sound, like wind, but different. And the small, sharp crackling of fire in grass. She felt the heat from it. She tried to see. The wind shifted the clouds of smoke.

She saw the fire then. A long crooked line of flames. Spreading straight toward her. A nearby stand of switchgrass flickered and fell away into smoking stalks. And then the smoke eclipsed the dark red line of flames.

"No . . . " She shook her head. "No . . . "

"Pa!" she screamed. "Ma!" But she knew she was way too far away from home for anyone to hear. A half-mile. Maybe more.

She could not go home now.

T HE RAVINE, THE CREEK must be on her left, but she would not go back into the ravine. The smoke there was thicker and she would lose her way. The smoke could suffocate her.

Plowed ground.

She had to get to plowed ground. She would stay on the prairie and go to plowed ground. The firebreaks the wagon man had burned. She'd be safe there. So she turned and ran blindly. Ran into the smoky world surrounding her. Ran, the heat and the wind on her back.

The smoke became ashy. Colleen's eyes and throat burned, and she tried to get air. She coughed. Behind her the steady wind whipped lurid flames across the tops of the grasses, burning them. And the fire spread forward.

Was O'Brien at the Stockdale cabin with Bonnie now? Was O'Brien watching out for Bonnie? Was he watching out for sparks? Because this ash, this ash could drift anywhere. And start a fire . . . *Ring the cowbell if you see any you can't put out.* . . . Did the wagon man know he was supposed to watch for sparks? Watch Bonnie and put out any sparks?

Or had he left? Because of the fire. Taken Bonnie and left.

Colleen stumbled along, coughing, trying to catch her breath. Behind her, the smoky line of red flames moved closer. Taller now. Taller than her head. In front of her, she saw something dark. The firebreaks. It must be the firebreaks. Now she'd be safe. She ran harder.

But there was nothing ahead of her. She ran and nothing was there. Just dry grass. Just smoke. No firebreaks. She stopped, and turned around and around looking. She couldn't even see the fire. Just smoke.

The wind blew her hair, pressed hard on her face and it gave her direction. But the fire *moved* with that wind. So she ran. She told herself she was almost there, almost to where the wagon man and those river men had plowed the furrows. The fire could not burn there between those furrows.

Suddenly Colleen stopped, stumbling to her knees, staring ahead of her.

Something was wrong. Something was terribly wrong.

Flames. A little line of flames in *front* of her. How did she get turned around? The wind? Was it shifting direction? She looked over her shoulder and then she knew. There was fire over her shoulder too. And she knew.

The man, the wagon man, he had started a backfire. Just like Pa. To meet the fire.

The backfire would run into the fire on the prairie. And she was caught between the two lines of fire.

Ⅰ N A SECOND, COLLEEN looked toward the ravine. In a second, she started running toward the ravine. The backfire would burn slowly toward the north. Now she had to get around that backfire . . . over toward the broken ground near the ravine where the fire would die out.

She ran so fast, so fast. The smoke was too thick. It was choking her. She kept running, running. She hurt all over. Her legs, her throat, her eyes.

She was going to smother in this smoke. It would get thicker and thicker and she would not be able to find any air left mixed in with it and she would smother.

But Colleen came to shrubs, a yucca. She was at the break.

Colleen could get around the backfire now. She made her way across the broken ground beside the ravine, and she ran again toward wide furrows she knew surrounded the old cabin. That was where Bonnie must be.

Unless the wagon man had left.

Finally Colleen was there. She fell down into deeply

tilled earth. Cool, soft earth. She lay there on her side, her hair, her hands, herself on the cool, soft, plowed earth. It was easier to breathe so close to the ground. She closed her eyes and breathed in the deep smell of the dirt. It smelled crisp and cold, like autumn.

Colleen opened her eyes. She lay very still.
Then up on her knees, she dusted off her hands,
pushed her hair off her face. Out on the prairie O'Brien's
backfire met the prairie fire. The grasses there flamed,
brilliant and tall, and then turned to smoke.

Colleen sat back on her heels and looked around. The
wagon was off a ways behind her. And further the old
cabin, the barn. Clay O'Brien's figure, small in the distance, was walking toward the buildings. Colleen heard
Bonnie start crying, only to stop. Several times. Bonnie
was there in the cabin. Bonnie was hungry. She must be
all right. She must be.

Colleen looked across the smoking prairie, across
blackened stalks where the wild grasses had been, to
shrubs and yuccas growing by the ravine.

Something caught her eye.

She had been here . . . right here. In this place.

She had seen a crouching cat. The shape of a giant
crouching cat. She'd seen it the night of the storm.

But that was clouds. . . . She had *thought* that was

clouds . . . yet here it was, the same shape, in the tops of cottonwoods edging above the rim of the ravine.

Could it be?

Could it be this is what she saw that night when Shine bolted? It *must* be. It had to be.

Those were *cottonwoods* she saw that night. Not clouds.

It was *here* that Shine spooked. Colleen stood up.

Maybe this was where the box fell off. When Shine reared! She took a step backward, squinting. Her heartbeat quickened.

Now the grass could not hide a box that fell off a horse. . . .

The grass was gone.

Colleen started walking out on the smoking prairie looking. The wind was steady, the smoke clearing some.

She remembered something else. Running after Shine. Something had tripped her. Right around here.

Colleen started walking faster, looking. A skeleton of an old dead cottonwood. Mostly a log. A few branches. Sun bleached, now scorched and smoking. She stooped down and touched it. Maybe what tripped her.

She stood up and looked across the seared earth.

Something small. Like a box. She took a step toward it.

Colleen ran. She ran, and there in the smoking stalks, no longer hidden, Colleen found the box.

Out on the prairie the rippling line of fire moved on. Beyond it, beyond its smoke, pushed on by the strong wind Colleen thought she saw touches of the autumn golds and maroons.

COLLEEN CAME AGAIN to the firebreak, and the Indian grass and switchgrass beyond it spread before her, muted by smoke, but still golden and untouched by the fire. O'Brien's two horses stood silently in front of the cabin. The black was still saddled, and the Appaloosa raised its head watching her. She clutched the metal box to her chest and waited for only a moment before running toward the cabin.

"Mr. O'Brien!" Colleen screamed. The heavy box fell from her arms to the ground, and Colleen bent to pick it up. "Mr. O'Brien!"

She saw him at the door of the cabin, watching her. "Look, Mr. O'Brien! I have the money. I have it!" she called.

Colleen handed him the box and followed him inside. The cabin was cool.

Her eyes skittered about the dim room. There was but one small window, so grungy no clear light came through. A pale blue bundle on a small bed in the dark corner. Colleen ran to Bonnie. Bonnie was sleepy and

Colleen gathered her in her arms, moving the pale blue blanket away from Bonnie's face. "Hey, baby," Colleen said, and Bonnie smiled at her.

Clay O'Brien had put the box on a rough, badly stained ash table. A haversack was packed and lay beside the Springfield rifle near the door.

O'Brien took a key from his shirt pocket and opened the box, fumbled with the money inside, counting it. He turned and looked at Colleen.

"It was out there," Colleen said. "It was out there, hidden in the grass . . . but the fire . . . " She took a breath. "I found it after the fire came through."

"You didn't have this . . . ?"

Colleen shook her head. But O'Brien was looking at the money. "No," she said. "Except that night. Your wife told me to take it. I lost it . . . in the storm."

"Kathleen told you to take it all? She had no right . . ." He looked up at her. His eyes were that deep shimmering blue and his voice, weary. "It was my money. Did you know that?" He seemed to be waiting.

And Colleen guessed that she knew, she guessed that she did. And she started to say that. But he waved his hand, shook his head, dismissed her from any need to answer.

She could take Bonnie now?

She could not say the words.

Clay O'Brien pulled out two rolls of bills, wrapped in twine, tossed them on the table. "The money you gave me the other day, it's there."

Colleen hesitated.

"It's yours. Take it," the wagon man said.

Colleen moved to the table and took the money. She stuffed it in her pocket. The widow's money. And Pa and Ma's. *I don't steal,* she had said to the man one summer day. She could not say that now. She would take the widow's back once she got Bonnie home. She would have to tell the widow what she did.

She stepped back, watching the man, one hand cradling Bonnie's head. He riffled through the money from the box, looked at Colleen again. His eyes returned to the box, and Colleen waited. Outside, Colleen heard one of the horses blowing. And finally Clay O'Brien talked, his eyes still on the table and the box. "That old nag, take her to that boy . . . and Kathleen told you to keep the young'un. I got no use for her."

Colleen saw a light in O'Brien's eyes. A shadow of something good. Fleeting as a lone feather caught on a blade of grass, waiting for a sure wind. Colleen looked at O'Brien, not knowing what to say then and so said nothing.

She carried Bonnie to the door and stopped. She looked around. "It's a good horse for my brother."

The man looked up. And then nodded his head. "You go on home, McCall girl."

Colleen left the cabin. She glanced at Bonnie, and Bonnie made a humming sound and began to suck her thumb. Through the door she could see the wagon man. He had taken up the haversack and put it on the table. Colleen took the reins of the old Appaloosa. And started walking.

She could go home and never say another word. She knew that. But no. She didn't want to keep the secret anymore. She wanted Ma and Pa to know. No matter what.

Colleen turned back and saw the man was outside. The black mare moved about uneasily and the man was rubbing her neck, settling her. Colleen watched them, filtered through hazy trails of smoke drifting, and she turned and walked for home, leading the old dappled horse and carrying the baby. She came to the freshly plowed firebreaks and crossed them and walked again on charred ground, in the smoking wild grass stalks, to the old wagon. Mary Kathleen's wagon. Sparks had caught there on the dry wood of the wheel, and were slowly burning, not having reached the canvas yet.

Colleen waited. A flicker became a curling flame and touched the canvas burning brightly. Colleen circled the wagon and when she looked up again the wagon was afire.

She walked toward home then with her baby sister and a horse the color of smoke.

She did not wait to see the wagon sag and fall away but left it ablaze, bright once again like the time she first saw it in the grass it had once sailed across . . .

Discussion Questions

(page numbers are in parentheses)

1. What did you like about this book? What kept you reading?

2. What characteristics would you use to describe Colleen McCall? How is she a typical twelve-year-old?

3. How does the author build suspense, both leading up to and following the switch of babies?

4. Mary Kathleen believes providence sends Colleen to her, and Colleen comes to believe it herself. However, when she decides not to tell, she does so "on her own"(22). Do you think Colleen thinks about God when she makes her decision? Is her family very religious? How does this affect her decision?

5. Why does Colleen give in to the wagon woman's demands? Colleen believes, "There was surely no promise more important than one made to somebody dying"(48). Do you agree? Later on, she thinks, "She should have told Ma and Pa. Even if they hated her. She was just so afraid and she had promised"(170). What does a promise mean to Colleen? To you? Does keeping your word mean more than following the law?

6. What keeps Colleen from telling her parents the truth? What assumptions does Colleen make about her parents' reaction? About Mr. O'Brien? How do these assumptions end up hurting the McCalls? Why is that ironic?

7. Define a lie. How does Colleen's attitude toward lying change throughout the novel? Colleen thinks, "She had always been an honest girl. *Always*. And this about Bonnie . . . that wasn't the same as real lying"(63). Do you agree? Are some lies okay?

8. Do you agree with Colleen's decision to switch the babies? To not tell her parents? Discuss Colleen's values. Why do you agree or disagree with them?

Literary Devices

1. "The backfire would run into the fire on the prairie. And she was caught between the two lines of fire"(174). How can this statement be understood as a metaphor of Colleen's conflict throughout the novel?

2. What significance does time have in the novel? How is the prairie both a timeless place and a place where time is most important? Colleen often thinks, "It seemed the wrong time"(164). How is time measured?

3. What does the wagon represent to Colleen? Both she and the wagon woman see the other as their salvation—does this change by the end of the story, or has this been a saving experience for Colleen?

4. Authors sometimes use personification, a literary device, to give inanimate objects human characteristics. How does the author personify the prairie?

5. What is the meaning of the title, *Prairie Whispers*? How are whispers significant throughout the book?

Further Exploration

1. Write in an essay about what you would do in Colleen's shoes. What factors play into your decision? What are the consequences of your choices?

2. Discuss metaphors as characters. What metaphors are used in the book that affect Colleen's decision? Select an object and, in an essay, identify the properties of the object that parallel her inner turmoil.

3. Daily life in the 1860s was completely different from daily life now. Compare your family's chore list to the McCall family's. Discuss which chores are harder and why.

4. Find the passages that describe the changing of seasons. How does the McCall family change each season? How do the seasons correspond to Colleen's mood? Write an essay on one season— what it has been known to represent, and what it represents for Colleen.

5. Look at a copy of Harvey Dunn's painting *In Search of the Land of Milk and Honey*. Write your own imagined story of the painting.